The Dean's Wife and Three Young Curates

The Dean's Wife and Three Young Curates

Sydney James

Matchstick Literary
1-888-306-8885
orders@matchliterary.com

Primary Characters in This Story

The dean's wife
The Revd Brian Braithwaite
The Revd Charles Huskins
The Revd Alex Bates

Secondary Characters

The dean
Sally, Brian's wife
Angela, Charles's wife
Alice, Alex's housekeeper
Dan, the motel owner

Minor Characters

Fr Carlos Resendez
The prison warden
Nicholas, Brian's son
Georgina, Brian's daughter

THE COVER STORY

THE COVER IMAGES denote the central characters in the story. The dean's wife leads the three young curates into her life of sexual gratification. This is represented by the dog collars. The clerical 'dog collars' signify an outward sign of church ethics except these are not spiritually understood by many, least of all the fictitious characters, demonstrated by their secular lifestyle.

Events take place towards the end of the twentieth century in the diocese of a major city, which could be anywhere in the Western Christian world. It's a torrid tale of questionable ethics, seduction and sexual excess, leading to crime and finally spiritual redemption. The church embedded includes the body of the church as well as the hierarchy of the Institution.

Their lives appear acceptable in a church lacking accountability. Sin is an acceptable indiscretion, not just for themselves, but also for those with whom they associate both inside the church as well as in the wider community. The young men don't consider themselves sinless, they simply have their own understanding of a world in which anything biblically sinful does not apply today. Their understanding of Christianity overlooks the difference between judgment by man rather than judgment by God. The story shows a side of Christianity, which is more about 'churchianity' meaning those who consider themselves Christian simply because they attend church on Sunday, but live a secular lifestyle from Monday to Saturday.

As the story unfolds it becomes evident the seemingly Christian structure of society is inextricably interwoven with the secular, so much so it becomes difficult to discern one from the other. This reality is shown in the fictitious character's behavior, whose experience leads them to transgressions with serious consequences. These affect not only immediate and extended family, but also subsequent generations. As the story unfolds, church and secular transgressions show how man (and woman) can momentarily fall, followed by a lifetime of anxiety, emotional pain, and even physical illness.

INTRODUCTION

ONE OF HUMANKIND'S primal instincts is the sex drive. Unlike the animal kingdom, in which procreation is the primary objective in survival of the fittest, human instincts are motivated by pleasure, lust, appetite, and personal gratification within the boundaries of choice. Of course, there is also what might be considered a side effect for some, resulting in procreation—except in reality, this is usually low on the agenda of most experiences of human sexual intercourse. More often than not, those involved in the experience have absolutely no desire to procreate, and measures are taken to prevent pregnancy.

These instincts are played out in all these boundaries between the various characters in the story. They are not confined to heterosexual relationships, except the motivational instincts are similar in character.

PROLOGUE

THE REVEREND BRIAN Braithwaite suddenly awoke in a state of shock, wondering where he was. After rubbing the sleep out of his eyes, he scanned his surroundings, accepting the familiarity of where he was—in bed with the dean's wife! As he lay there reflecting on the circumstances which had led to this situation, he was amazed how quickly his entire life flashed through his mind in just a few moments. In reality, it represented almost twenty-five years. He forced himself out of his reverie, realising he'd never actually fallen asleep after one of these sexual encounters before, and the urge to get himself together and out of there was becoming urgent.

He wasn't concerned the dean might suddenly return home, because he was overseas on one of his lecturing tours. But without instantly knowing the time of day or night, as well as perhaps where he should be instead of where he was, he was trying to get his mind into gear.

PROLOGUE

CHAPTER ONE

THE RECESS BELL echoed round the quadrangle as kids poured out of their classrooms like a nest of ants after something to eat. It wasn't raining, so they quickly organised themselves to play marbles, hopscotch, rope-skipping, and a variety of ball games. Brian watched, curiously inept at the boredom of this repetitive scene.

He noticed a short stocky boy standing close, similarly disinterested in playing. 'Hi, my name's Brian. I see you're not interested in these stupid games either.'

'No,' the boy replied.

'I'm in class 5A and like geography and history,' Brian continued. 'What subjects do you like best?'

'None.'

'What's your name?' Brian realised anything beyond a single-word reply was unlikely.

'Alex,' was all he offered.

Another boy drifted towards them. Brian redirected his attention.

'Hi, my name's Brian,' he tried again. But before he could say any more, he was interrupted.

'Charles, and I'm in 5B, pretty much in the middle stream.'

'So what subjects do you like?' Brian managed to get a word in.

'I seem to be okay at most subjects and don't really have any favourites.'

'This is Alex,' said Brian. 'He's not interested'—and he was about to say *in anything*, but checked himself—'in any of the stupid games either.'

Even as young boys, it seemed clear they weren't about to become close friends, but they gravitated towards each other in the playground, sensing a common interest of being different from everyone else. As a consequence, a trust was spawned during early childhood. They shared things important to them as boys—things they felt unable to share with teachers, parents, or even other children. These childhood issues were important to them, insignificant to others.

Brian Braithwaite was a confident boy and became the self-appointed leader of his two new friends. He listened to them and gave advice. He felt proud to counsel them, and it made him feel important.

Charles Huskins was quietly confident but kept his opinions to himself. Nobody ever called him Charlie; it just didn't suit him. He was definitely a Charles. He was a thinker and rarely contributed to discussions between his two friends. He was happy to listen and occasionally nod his head in agreement.

The third member of the group, Alex Bates, was a misfit. He had few social skills. He was always seeking support from his two friends. He misunderstood or reacted negatively to just about anything. This fed his insecurity and continually destroyed what little self-esteem he had.

There was another boy hanging around who appeared disinterested in joining games. He stood alone but in earshot, close enough to hear the group of three but keeping a comfortable distance. He was also different, presenting a serious demeanour.

Brian extended his usual invitation. 'Hi, my name's Brian. What's yours?'

There was no reply. The boy seemed nervous.

Brian tried again. This time the boy managed a response. 'Me no Engleesh, me Carlos!'

So Brian got the message the boy was a new immigrant. *No point in trying to talk to him if he can't understand.*

CHAPTER TWO

B RIAN'S EYES WANDERED around the room and came back to the dean's wife lying beside him, still asleep, so serene and remarkably beautiful. Her skin tone was perfect, and tiny drops of perspiration on her forehead sparkled like dew. His pride led him to believe he'd something sexual to offer which nobody else could. He was naive as well as proud. *How on earth did I get into this situation? Not that I'm complaining.*

His wife Sally's choice of bed linen was nothing fancy; she bought whatever was on sale. The dean's wife had peach-coloured silk sheets, matching her skin colour. Every movement he made between the sheets was like a caress from her naked body. He moved his legs around and felt the sensation of the sheets. His movement brought her out of her slumber. She turned to face him, and as she opened her eyes, Brian knew he wouldn't be leaving just yet. 'What are you thinking?' she asked smiling.

Brian had lost count how many times he'd been in bed with her. He wanted to say, 'Aren't you ever satisfied?' He knew she wanted more, so he followed her lead. He'd developed verbal responses which were never truthful, and he quickly thought of something else to say.

'Just wondering how you're able to keep such a beautiful complexion'—*at your age,* he thought but didn't say. 'I was admiring your silky smooth skin as you slept.' *Nearly put my foot in it there!*

As the sheets billowed, the exotic aroma of her perfume (reminiscent of the first time he'd met her) wafted under his nose. It was intoxicatingly seductive. She had an insatiable appetite for sex, and Brian wasn't about to deny her desires. Well, he never had before.

This time she wanted complete control and settled herself on top of him, leading their intercourse. Brian's previous sexual experience had been limited. He'd thought there was only one position to have sex.

He was embarrassed by the squeals and screams of the dean's wife as sensuous feelings rose and fell.

'Let yourself go, Brian!'

'What do you mean?' He was willing to learn but confused.

'Speak to me, tell me what you're feeling.' *I'm putting in all the effort, and you're just a sex machine!*

This was part of Brian's inexperience, and she wanted him to talk dirty. *Something else I'll have to teach him.*

It wasn't as if anyone would hear them. It was simply something he was unfamiliar with. He was familiar with one position, one speed, all done in silence and usually in darkness with similarly inexperienced partners. His sexual horizon had been pushed far beyond his imagination during their relationship.

'How do you like it this way?' She tried again as she recovered her breath. It wasn't as if it was hard work, but the effort was one-sided.

The spontaneity of his response was truthful this time as he said, 'I've never had it this way before.' His thoughts were of the silky sheets beneath him and the silky body on top of him. As always, his mind disengaged with his bodily functions.

Because he wasn't leading, he reflected once again upon his circumstances. His mind drifted away even though he was having an extraordinary sexual experience. He thought his background influenced the way his life had developed. He came from a middle-class family, both parents working full-time in a professional capacity. His father was a surveyor and his mother, a librarian; and because he'd no brothers or sisters, it gave him a special upbringing as an only child. He'd have described himself as above average at school and later at university, where he'd studied for an arts degree without really having any career ambition. Pride drove his thoughts at this time, when perhaps he should be more engaging with the dean's wife gyrating on top of him.

Brian thought she might be tiring as she moved from lying on him to sitting on him. Her breasts were relatively small, certainly not big, and he became hypnotised as he watched them wobble.

'Hold them for me,' she said, and as usual, he complied with her every request. Brian's compliance was all part of her teaching process.

Perhaps as a reflection of his upbringing, he was tidy, almost clinical. He'd fairly short dark hair, blue eyes, and a physique to position him above the norm. Six feet two and ninety-five kilos made him a natural selection for sport, except he was disinterested in contact sport, as he was in almost any other sport. He could watch it with mild enthusiasm, but the idea of supporting any particular team was well outside his level of interest. Cricket, on the other hand, mildly attracted him, and he'd been the self-appointed opening batsman at school and later in club cricket.

But this was a whole different ball game. He relaxed in the comfort of her bed, with a willing and experienced partner having a feminine appetite hitherto beyond his imagination. Limitless time—well, almost—and endless enthusiasm.

CHAPTER THREE

Brian Braithwaite

Brian's family background as an only child had been comfortable. He certainly didn't always have his own way, but his needs were met and he never went without. This applied to food, toys, clothes, and love. His parents encouraged him to try harder at school. He was a good scholar.

'Good marks mean a good job,' his father said.

So he achieved, got good marks, and felt pride.

Brian was almost head and shoulders above other kids of his age. He stood out in a group of children. He had confidence and social skills even in childhood. He always sat at the front of the class and was noticed by his teachers.

Charles Huskins

He had an older sister whom he hardly ever saw and had no family relationship with her. Charles was a natural learner and, without much effort, picked up almost any subject and achieved middle grades through basic schooling. In fact, he could have been quite a scholar if he'd put a bit more effort into learning, but it wasn't in his nature.

Charles always positioned himself in the middle of the classroom and was often thought to be absent when, in fact, he was present. He was the sort of child nobody noticed: average height, average weight, average—average! He did, however, stand out annually in the school's cross-country run. There was no reason for him to associate with Brian or Alex other than perhaps his dislike of contact sport and, of course, ball games.

Alex Bates

Alex was one of four siblings (two older brothers and a younger sister), and he always lived in hand-me-downs, clothes or toys. His parents were never involved in school activities and had no idea where he fitted into A or B grades. In fact, he was always in the bottom-C grade and had no understanding of what went on in the classroom. He simply turned up and sat at the back of the class. If the teacher asked him a question, he mumbled his way through, and teachers quickly gave up even trying to teach him anything.

Alex was short for his age with broad shoulders. He looked a bit of a tough guy, ready for a fight, but this wasn't in his nature. He was polite and never answered back, but his communication skills were limited; he felt embarrassed to speak to anyone other than his two special friends, Brian and Charles. He'd an idea of what to say but was unable to articulate the words quickly enough to gain attention.

One of the kids tried to include Alex in a game. 'Come on then. Throw the ball back and make a doubles team with me.'

Alex struggled to decline the invitation. 'Thanks, but I . . .' Even when he tried, he found that other kids would turn away before he'd finished what he was trying to say. This made him a bit of a social outcast as well as fed his insecurity. He was slow to think of an excuse instead of simply saying 'No, thanks'.

He'd struggled with reading and writing but had practical attributes. If he was shown how to do something, he could replicate the instruction.

Alex also found it difficult to speak to his parents—not just because there were other siblings fighting for attention, but also because he'd difficulty arranging his mind in order to get the words out even at home, by which time one of his brothers or sister had parental attention.

'How was school today?' his mum would ask.

'Okay.'

'So what did you do today?'

'Nothing much.'

'What's your teacher's name?'

'Don't know.'

As a consequence, he became a recluse, always turning inwards to deal with issues he was unable to articulate. He found it much easier talking to Brian.

'I'm always happy to listen to you, Alex, if I can help and give you some advice,' Brian would always encourage.

Alex was unable to follow what was sometimes considered to be a joke, maybe even at his expense. One of the things that made the whole class laugh apart from him was when the teacher called out his name.

'Master Bates!'

Alex withdrew into his own world at times like this. If he was the subject of a joke he didn't understand, it made him feel inadequate. These things made him feel different from everyone else and isolated him from all the kids, apart from Brian and Charles.

Carlos Resendez

Even though he couldn't understand the language, Carlos lingered next to the group of three. He picked up the odd word. He was one of a large Spanish family who'd sent him to school, where they'd hoped he'd learn English. His mother had an Irish background with Catholic values. Nobody actually taught Carlos English. He was left to his own devices to learn from other kids.

Brian shared his thoughts with his two friends. 'It's not his fault he can't speak English.'

'I guess not, but it's not our job to teach him,' said Alex.

'Well, there's no harm in trying. How's he going to learn otherwise?' Charles chipped in.

'Well, don't ask me to do it,' said Alex. 'I have my own problems trying to talk to people.'

Carlos continued to hang around, sometimes saying one or two words and getting quickly corrected for pronunciation. He was a good-looking lad of slight build with olive skin, dark hair, and brown eyes; and he was always polite. Brian tried speaking to him again. 'Do you have any brothers and sisters, Carlos?'

'Me four brudders.' Carlos tried his English and was quickly corrected. He didn't mind. How else was he to learn?

So here were four adolescents, similar in some ways (they all had two of everything they were supposed to have) but very different in character, ability, nature, and ethnicity. It was an association based entirely on need.

CHAPTER FOUR

BRIAN'S THOUGHTS DRIFTED back to his first visit to the deanery, where he'd become more familiar with the dean's wife. It seemed a lifetime ago. There'd been about twelve guests, including his two friends Alex and Charles, who by then had also been deaconed. They'd lost touch with Carlos. Family ties were stronger than friendship in his ethnic community.

The deanery was a formal residence of distinction, well-furnished and comfortable. Brian remembered feeling out of place; it didn't have that feeling of being a family home. The dean's wife had employed a catering contractor and was free to entertain her guests. She obviously knew everyone and fluttered around like a social butterfly. As expected, the chat was formal and restrained, nothing risqué.

Brian was seated next to the dean's wife, and her perfume triggered his hormonal senses. He kept checking his position in his chair. A big space between the dinner guest on his right and almost no space between him and the dean's wife to his left! The chairs were actually touching, so Brian couldn't move his chair away; it was the position of bums on seats only that offered some movement.

He'd felt reasonably comfortable during the first course, smoked salmon on little rye bread fingers. He watched the dean's wife delicately sample a finger of bread and dip the salmon into some sort of mayonnaise sauce garnished with chopped dill. He watched as she placed it gently in her mouth and unconsciously gasped out loud as her tongue rolled over her lips to remove some mayonnaise from her upper lip.

He quickly checked his behaviour as well as the space between him and the dean's wife, hoping nobody had noticed his exclamation or the proximity of his body next to her. He was captivated and suddenly felt he was the only other person at the table. He composed himself as the entrée was cleared away. *Get a grip on yourself. It's just a dinner party. What am I thinking? What am I feeling?*

'Did you enjoy the entrée, Brian?' she said. But he couldn't remember eating any. He'd become so engrossed by her closeness. He reached for his glass of wine and gulped it down in a single swallow as if it were water.

'Lovely,' he replied, hoping he'd actually eaten what was on the plate the waiters had just taken away. *What an idiot! I've just said it was lovely and can't remember if I ate any of it. Get a grip on yourself,* he told himself again.

The next course arrived and was carved at the table, an eye fillet of beef. The choice was well done one end of the joint, medium at the other, and rare in the middle. The waiter served.

'Would you care for some beef, sir?' the waiter enquired.

'Oh yes, thank you,' Brian replied.

'Would you like it rare, medium rare, or well done, sir?'

'I beg your pardon.' *What are you talking about?*

'The beef, sir, would you like it from the middle of the cut or from either end?'

'Sorry,' said Brian. 'Medium rare please.' This was going to be a long meal. His concentration kept wandering.

The knees of the dean's wife gently touched Brian's knees, and every time this happened, he checked his position again in his chair. He remeasured the distance between the person on his right, consciously trying to balance the distance between himself and the dean's wife on the other side. Charles was at the other end of the table and seemed to be engrossed in discussion with the dean. He wondered what they were talking about since he wasn't aware they'd anything in common, apart from the church, of course!

Alex wasn't talking to anyone and seemed to be enjoying copious amounts of food and wine. This completely occupied his time and effort. *No need to talk with all this good food around,* thought Alex. He was able to exchange a few words between mouthfuls, except every time he took even a sip of wine, a waiter refilled his glass. *I might get to like the church if this is the sort of food we get,* thought Alex.

At the other end of the table, the knees of Brian and the dean's wife touched too often to be accidental, and when she placed her hand on his knee, he was overcome with embarrassment as well as desire. *What the hell am I supposed to do now?* he thought. It seemed an eternity before the vegetables arrived, during which she was gently caressing the inside of his thigh from knee to groin, pausing at the groin. The look in her eyes suggested, *I don't have to stop here!*

'The dean brought this wine back from one of his overseas trips,' she announced to everyone. 'It's a Pinot Noir, a deliciously light red wine, which compliments red meat so wonderfully, don't you think?'

Brian's linguistic skills were now reduced to single words. 'Absolutely.' *Wasn't anyone else going to say anything about the wine?* He was beginning to think he'd already had enough to drink—a glass of champagne with canapés, two glasses of white, and one glass of red. *Or have I lost count?* He was losing his diction as well as his mind in what to say, let alone what to do! *Why couldn't someone else talk to me around the table?* He learnt the only way to stop waiters from refilling his glass was not to drink at all. Even a sip prompted the wine waiters into the action of refilling. Alex clearly liked this idea, except he seemed to be able to hold his drink without saying anything embarrassing. Then again, he wasn't speaking, just eating and drinking. And he wasn't sitting next to the dean's wife!

The man on his right was so engrossed in discussion with the lady on the other side, his back half turned towards Brian. There was no prospect of having any discussion with him. Brian's only escape would be to sit on half of his chair. He was trapped between the guy's back and the dean's wife. He thought of perhaps excusing himself from the table and going to find a toilet but dismissed the thought because he might get lost or, even worse, fall over, feeling more than slightly intoxicated.

'You'll love the dessert, Brian,' she said. 'It's something I created myself and got the chef to prepare for us. It's fresh mango slices garnished with passion fruit and homemade ice cream. It's so exotic.' *Or did she say* erotic? Brian even doubted what he was hearing, and he certainly doubted what he was feeling under the table.

'There's a beautiful selection of soft cheeses,' the dean's wife announced after dessert. 'I recommend the ripe Camembert. It has a sexy aroma, and I'd love to know what the smell reminds you of.'

She wasn't really expecting any response, but having had a few drinks herself, she simply stirred up Brian's juices; she was starting to be more openly provocative.

'Coffee is served in the drawing room,' announced the head waiter. Brian needed to wait for guests and especially the dean's wife to move away from table because his erection would have been noticeable. He sat quietly for a while. Alex came up to encourage him to go into the next room for coffee.

'Great dinner,' said Alex.

Alex didn't much like shopping or cooking, but he did like eating almost as much as he liked drinking. The more the better, and he'd had second helpings of every course as it was offered. Why refuse? He was totally oblivious to everyone else declining on the grounds of politeness.

'Yes, and the company was good,' said Charles, wanting to question Brian's obvious embarrassment. 'You seemed to be getting along famously with the dean's wife. What on earth were you talking about all the time?'

'Can't remember,' said Brian.

'It was only five minutes ago,' challenged Alex. 'What's the big secret?'

If only you knew, thought Brian.

CHAPTER FIVE

THE DEAN'S WIFE was a stunningly attractive mature woman. It was difficult to guess her age. The dean was in his mid fifties, but it didn't mean she was the same age. She could easily have been ten years younger—she certainly looked it. She always dressed in what Brian described as a little black cocktail dress. It was very slimming, and the hem was just above the knee and swung provocatively with her hips as she made entry into a crowded room. Her figure was well proportioned, and the absence of any bulges in the wrong places suggested she took care of herself. She could have graced the front page of many a fashion magazine, having high cheekbones and a peaches-and-cream complexion gently framed by her short honey-blonde hair.

Her most striking feature however (at least to Brian) were her eyes, except not so much the colour as the expression she was able to convey by a glance or an enquiring look. Her eyes asked questions that were beyond words, and Brian's first reaction was to look away. He was so inexperienced at seduction. The rest of her attire was always immaculate in matching shoes and modest make-up. Brian wondered if she looked at every man in such a provocative manner.

He convinced himself she'd be viewed by every man with the same desire, except it was his knees and thighs she'd caressed under the table. So it was irrelevant what any other man might have felt, because it was only he who had the feeling, and what a feeling it was!

During dinner the dean had tapped his glass with a spoon to make an announcement. 'I shall be going overseas again next week on one of my lecturing tours. A number of churches have requested I address them—one in particular has invited me to make the keynote address at their annual conference.' Everyone applauded.

After the guests had gone, the dean gave instructions to his wife. 'I am interested in Brian as my possible successor. I'd like you to introduce him to the lifestyle of high office.' Of course, it wasn't the dean's role to appoint his successor, but this showed his desire for control.

'Anything in particular?' she enquired.

'No, I'll leave it to you. I'm sure you can think of the sort of things that would attract him to become more active in the hierarchy of the church.'

'I think I know what you mean.' *I have a few ideas already*, she thought.

Of course, the dean probably meant things like the house, the furniture, and the well-appointed study (surely not the bedroom). However, during one of Brian's several visits to the deanery, things were clearly developing from ground level to the first floor. The black cocktail dress wasn't worn at home, replaced by slacks and blouse—buttons positioned to leave little to the imagination. Bra-less at home was probably normal and even acceptable, but not when receiving guests. Definitely not when receiving an unaccompanied young male guest. However, as these house visits became more frequent, the attire became even more casual and revealing in the form of a loose silk housecoat. Not only bra-less but also knicker-less!

Brian became comfortable, even at home with the quality of the house and contents, so this wasn't in itself embarrassing. But the direction the relationship was heading was obvious, and Brian struggled with taking the next step. He thought it would be his choice if matters were to proceed.

It wasn't the first time they'd been upstairs together as the dean's study was on the first floor, which included a respectable library of both theological and classic books. Brian had been encouraged to access and borrow at his discretion. The bedroom was next door, and they'd drifted in so casually Brian hardly realised he'd followed her in.

The dean's wife came quickly to the point. 'Would you like to have sex?' she asked in a matter-of-fact tone.

'Look, I don't really think I should.'

'I didn't ask you if you should, I asked if you'd like to.'

Brian usually liked to think things through, but he could see a window of opportunity which wasn't going to stay open for long. Before he responded, he tried to weigh up the positives and negatives, but desire overwhelmed him.

'Sure,' he said, but he thought, *Why not. It's being handed to me on a plate. Opportunities like this don't happen every day of the week. In fact, they've never happened to me before.*

Brian suddenly found himself out of his depth. He'd never had sex with a mature woman, and his immaturity was very evident to the dean's wife. She tried to slow things down, but he only had one speed, straight into top gear. It became a mixture of frustration and inexperience. Brian had just got going when she would change positions. In his limited experience, he was used to a single sexual position, but she had so many options he was becoming exhausted. He'd heard about these situations but thought they were optimistic fantasies by fiction writers, except it was actually happening to him now. He was being led, and she took control. Ultimately, he was unable to hold on any longer, and the explosion of ejaculation was more releasing of his stress and emotion than he'd ever experienced before.

'Did you enjoy it?' she said with a smile like a cat that'd just had the cream.

'Is the pope Catholic?' he replied, which upon reflection was probably not the most appropriate thing to have said. He quickly followed it up. 'Yes, absolutely fantastic!'

He almost said *thank you* but quickly checked himself. He was unable to notice her pleasure was in leading the inexperienced lover, and his malleability was what gave her pleasure. She was the teacher, and he was going to be her pupil. He needed much more tuition.

Brian couldn't help noticing as the passion unfolded that she seemed to be much more involved than he was. He was going through the motions, but he was more than a bit nervous—even distant. She was really enjoying it and took the lead all the time, showing him all sorts of nuances in sexual intercourse unknown to him. This slowed him down in his nervousness and fulfilled her confidence.

So that was how it all started for the Revd Brian Braithwaite, and here he was again, except it was by no means a limited encounter! He'd so much more to learn, and she'd so much more to teach.

CHAPTER SIX

AFTER GRADUATION FROM university and for reasons which could only be described as perfunctory, Brian decided to try and get a job with a company of architects, perhaps even to become an architect. Having applied for a few jobs in the city, he was surprised to get a response from Heddington, Heddington, and Boswell—a large company of architects employing about 180 people.

At his interview, he met with one of the partners, James Heddington, who was impressive, tall and trim, with greying hair at the temples. He was a well-dressed middle-aged man displaying a distinctive character of self-confidence. Brian couldn't help comparing his off-the-peg clothes with James Heddington's bespoke tailored suit. Quality oozed out of every pore of his body and made Brian feel inferior.

There'd been the usual pre-interview discussion to make Brian feel at ease, but he'd done a number of role-play interviews towards the end of his time at university. He introduced himself as James Heddington, but Brian addressed him as Mr Heddington. *Be respectful,* he remembered.

'So why do you want to be an architect?' enquired Mr Heddington.

He guessed this would be asked at some stage of the interview and was prepared with his answer having done some research on the Net. 'I believe architecture is much more than just about a building. Architecture plays a role not in self-glorification of the building but also in the achievement of other objectives within the building because it needs to inspire people.' *I think I remembered that correctly from the Internet.*

'What about design, Brian?'

'Yes, design's important too,' said Brian. 'We studied design, except however good the design, it has to be translated by a builder into structure, otherwise it's pie-in-the-sky stuff and it will just be a block of concrete.'

James Heddington was clearly impressed. 'I think you'll fit in very well here, Brian. We're a team at Heddingtons'. You start at the bottom, which is where we all start, so there's only one direction you can take from there—upwards.'

He was unable to suppress his pride having got a job with a prestigious firm of architects in his very first interview. Of course, pride was not limited to Brian. His parents soon shared the good news with everyone. For his part, Brian could now introduce himself to new acquaintances at his regular drinking hole, the Pig and Whistle, massaging his new career from 'working at Heddingtons' to 'being an architect at Heddingtons'. Just mention of the company name in any city hotel bar drew an appropriate response of recognition, and his pride rose to new heights.

Brian remembered his first day at Heddington's. Someone he hadn't met at interview, Mr Allan Jenkins, greeted him at reception and marched him through the office and up to a nineteen-inch monitor screen in a row of alcoves all looking much the same.

'Here's your workstation, Brian. It's a CADCAM machine. Settle in and have a play-around with it, and let's see what you can do. I'll be back later.'

I wonder what CADCAM *means? I guess it stands for something—just looks like a computer to me.* Brian eventually found the on switch, and a blank screen appeared. He could move the mouse around to drag lines around the screen. He became embarrassed by what appeared on the screen. Every time he clicked the mouse, another line appeared, and he couldn't delete anything. It looked like a juvenile doodle of crossed lines going nowhere, all different widths and lengths. *I can't see anything architectural in this by any stretch of my imagination, but then I had no idea what I was getting into.*

As the boredom of days passed, he learnt there were a number of other skills he didn't have, and they'd nothing to do with architecture. Departments had section leaders, assistant section leaders, and staff—he'd no idea how it all came together to effect an architectural result, but what the heck, he had a job. It was nine till five, and nobody seemed to care if he was learning CADCAM or not.

Occasionally someone would walk past his workstation and enquire how he was getting on. 'Hi, my name is Greg. You must be the new guy. How's it going, mate?'

Brian instinctively knew not to reply in truth. He responded, 'OK, thanks. It's all a bit new, but I'm getting there.'

For Brian, CADCAM started as being boring, and he never moved beyond that understanding. Each day became drudgery more meaningless than the last.

Everyone seemed to be after the job of his or her senior, and battle lines were drawn. If anyone could say something to discredit another, words were spoken in the appropriate ear so the grapevine could do its dirty work. Brian even became bored with telling people he met socially that he was an architect at Heddingtons'. The only good part was the weekly wage. Oh yes, and the coffee queue with girls.

The job enabled him to support himself modestly, because he was still living at home with his parents.

After his access to the coffee machine, the pool of prospective girls was the highlight of his day. There was one girl who always managed to be just behind him in the queue. He'd no idea what she did at Heddingtons' and didn't really care. It was her physical attributes that attracted him.

'Hi, my name's Sally. Do you ever get down to the Pig and Whistle?' she asked, as if she'd no idea where he spent almost every Saturday night.

'Yes, it's my regular watering hole, as a matter of fact,' said Brian. 'How about we meet there for a drink or something?' Brian was really angling for the something because Sally had the most gorgeous big tits and he couldn't wait to get his hands on them.

'Great then, I'll see you there tomorrow about seven o'clock p.m.,' said Brian as the queue moved slowly towards the coffee machine.

This development at work made all the difference, and it was not just Sally who'd excited him; there was a whole department of girls down one level. However, the boredom of the job eventually overcame his attraction to the girls.

He started to search for other job prospects but quickly came to the conclusion they were all basically the same if you had no skills to offer.

He knew his limitations even if nobody else did. His new girlfriend Sally was a Christian, and she tried to get him to go to church with her. In order to appear willing to do something she wanted, he decided to go along with her invitation because it might help him to achieve something he wanted her to do with him.

CHAPTER SEVEN

H E'D BEEN ATTRACTED to Sally because she stood out in a crowd. It wasn't only because she was well proportioned physically but also because her dress sense was unusual. She wore a mixture of styles and colours—not just slightly mismatched but grossly mismatched. It was not unusual for her to wear a lightweight pink polo-neck skivvy with an orange-coloured waistcoat and flaunting a bright-red scarf. This could be combined with a lime-green skirt and blue stockings. The skivvy could have had a sign on her chest saying, 'I'm not wearing a bra. Look how nicely my nipples stand out when you look at them.' The only things missing were tattoos, body piercings, and green hair.

As a couple, they drew attention to themselves in public, which clearly they both enjoyed. They liked to be noticed, to be the centre of attention and attract comment.

'That's Brian, the architect at Heddingtons', and his girlfriend, Sally. She's such a poseur!' he heard say as they entered the Pig and Whistle.

Brian was a 'short back and sides' guy and went to a barber, not a hairdresser. He was clean, smart, and indistinctive, unlike Sally, who always wanted to make a dress statement.

The difficulty for Brian was the next step. Should he come on to her? But what if he was rejected? Sally knew what she was doing, and like a flower to the bee, she'd sent her signals. Because she was a practicing Christian, she would hold her virginity for the man she would marry. Brian was unaware of this hurdle.

The attraction was, in fact, already well under way with her unusual attire, which had captured Brian's attention, except he was not so much interested in the wrapping as its contents.

'Will you come to church with me next Sunday?' Sally made her move.

'Yes, of course. What do I have to do? What should I say if people speak to me?'

'Just come and follow my lead. Most of it is just listening. Nothing to worry about.'

Well, Brian was worried, but what the heck. *I'll have to make some sacrifices if I'm to get in her knickers.*

'This week we're celebrating Holy Communion. You don't have to do it if you don't want to. The assistant minister is leading the service, and he's pretty new at it himself.' Sally encouraged Brian to relax. 'The dean is giving the sermon, and he's very good.'

There was structure to the service, and Brian listened with indifference to the sermon. It sounded very plausible. His interest wasn't so much the subject matter but more the absence of any reaction from the congregation. It was up to the individual how they might understand, accept, or even reject the subject matter. Nobody challenged or questioned anything the dean said.

Brian's thoughts reflected. *This is so different from the corporate world, where the need to continually achieve and progress through the ranks involves verbal confrontation, criticism, or disagreement. It's a veritable jungle out there in the survival of the strongest in character, not to mention ability. Church is interesting. This is so different.*

Brian looked around the church and noticed the featureless expression on everyone's face. There were no smiles, no tears, and they seemed to be empty shells of bodies with no expression—a load of zombies!

The pressure and stress at Heddingtons' had been relentless and played out as a sort of theatre where the office was the stage. There were times when he'd noticed the grapevine being fed by a couple in the coffee queue. He could've given them an Oscar for their performance. He'd wondered how anybody did any work. Apart from his own absence of contribution, he could only see this development of personal expression to influence the grapevine.

Not having anyone to talk to about a possible career redirection other than Sally, who was clearly biased, his mind drifted. *What's the point of staying at Heddingtons'? I'm a square peg in a round hole. They're going to find out pretty soon I can't operate CADCAM, whatever that is, and even if I could, what then? I can't come up with any ideas, apart from Sally. If I go to church with her, I'm not losing anything. I might even gain something.*

After the service, Brian and Sally joined the congregation for morning tea. Sally had introduced Brian to the dean and his wife.

'So what do you do for a crust?' the dean enquired of them both.

'We both work at Heddingtons', the architects in the city,' replied Sally.

The dean immediately jumped to the conclusion Brian was an architect before politely moving on to the next introduction. Brian's eyes lingered on the dean's wife. *What an attractive woman.*

CHAPTER EIGHT

A S BRIAN SAT at his workstation staring at CADCAM, he mused at having met the dean's wife. He was jolted out of his daydream.

'Hi, Brian, I'm Allan Jenkins, your section leader. Nice to see you again.'

'Howdy.' Brian was startled. *I've been employed here for six weeks, and this is the first time you've decided to come and see me.*

As if Jenkins had read his mind, the section leader said, 'I'm usually out on-site all day, and by the time I get into the office, everyone has gone. I'd like you to draw up a structural steel detail for a hotel. I need it manufactured and on-site within a couple of days, so consider it urgent.'

Jenkins presented some calculations on the back of a business card.

'An RSJ should meet the specification, but you'd better check to see if a W or a T profile might be stronger. You can check the calculations against the Euler–Bernoulli beam equation formula.'

Before Brian had time to draw breath and say, 'What on earth are you talking about?' Allan Jenkins was gone. He appeared from nowhere and disappeared to the same place just as quickly. Jenkins would doubtless be back soon not only wanting to know if the structure should be W or T profile but also wanting Brian to have produced a detail drawing off his CADCAM. The only thing Brian had learnt about CADCAM was it stood for 'computer-aided design/computer-aided manufacture'. He felt the pressure and stress build to an unbearable level. His mind collapsed. It was likely to happen more often. This was what the job was all about—actually producing something!

Everyone around was heads down, engrossed with the screen in front of them. He reacted to the confrontation in panic with negative thoughts.

The CADCAMs were all neatly arranged in a row as workstations. Unnamed people clicked away at their mouses. He wondered briefly why they were called mouses and not mice. The drone of fluorescent tubes humming overhead became deafening. He slowly stood, walked away from his workstation, went down one level, and got a coffee before walking out of Heddingtons', never to return. *What now?* he thought. The church beckoned!

He'd learnt from Sally that if he could become deaconed, the church would provide him a job immediately in a parish as a curate/assistant minister. *How difficult could it be?* His thoughts drifted back to his first church experience with Sally.

CHAPTER NINE

THE FRIENDSHIP BETWEEN Brian, Charles, and Alex took place with common purpose at the Pig and Whistle for a beer at weekends. It was the only time they could be themselves instead of putting on an act to parents, friends, or anyone else. They'd each developed a persona to present to others, a mask behind which to hide.

The lighting in the saloon bar was subdued, not dark, but facial expressions were almost invisible. A comforting smell of beer soaked into tables, chairs, and cushions and was a beacon that attracted every customer. They were in their comfort zone, their escape from the world outside. They each left their emotional baggage outside and became a natural person for a while. Other customers walked quietly past, either raising their glasses as acknowledgement of recognition or not. Strangers—just as welcome as friends.

There were loud voices in the public bar. A darts match was going on. The occasional cheer for a good score or raucous laughter if the dart missed the board altogether—all were part of the ambience contributing to pub life.

'Do you know why it's called the Pig and Whistle?' Charles asked one day when the discussion had drifted into a quiet spell.

'I've no idea. Nor do I care, so long as the beer's good and there's a log fire in the grate on these cold winter evenings,' responded Alex.

'Well, I'm interested, if you really know,' said Brian.

Charles continued. 'This whole area was notorious for law enforcement, so the police—pigs—were regularly involved. There weren't any mobile phones then, and they blew their whistles to call for help. Hence the pub got its name. Not many people know the origin. The old-timers in the public bar know and would tell anyone who stayed long enough to listen.'

'Okay, very interesting,' said Alex. 'Who's for another beer?'

The pub was where the threesome discussed their jobs and

expectations in life, not that Alex was very engaging in these discussions; after all, he was only there for the beer. Charles appreciated where Brian was leading. It wasn't as if Charles had no ambition. He just hadn't thought of a career as being much of a priority yet. Alex hadn't thought of it—period.

Allan Jenkins's demand for actual work had tipped Brian over the edge. It forced his hand to search for a career elsewhere, and the church's grass appeared greener on the other side. By his reckoning, it offered a number of advantages his architectural career was never likely to offer. He knew his limitations even if Heddingtons' didn't.

'I've been thinking about this for a while,' said Brian by way of introduction. 'I'm fed up with the rat race of corporate life. The church is different. I'm thinking of becoming a minister.'

Charles was quietly amused, and Alex nearly choked on his beer.

'You are joking, I hope,' said Alex when he'd recovered. 'What do you know about being a minister?'

'What's there to know, compared with being an architect?' Brian was at least able to say with some experience. 'I've been talking to Sally and have been to her church. There's nothing to it.'

Brian's beer glass was almost full, Charles's glass was half-full, and Alex's was empty again.

Alex jumped to his feet, 'I'll go and get another round, and perhaps you'll have come to your senses by the time I get back.'

'What was so difficult about Allan Jenkins wanting a drawing?' Charles wondered.

'I have no idea what a W or a T section is, how to design a drawing, or work a CADCAM system. They gave me no training and presumed I knew everything. It was boring, stressful, and had no future prospects.' Brian considered the subject closed.

'Anyway, I've left Heddingtons'. I couldn't stand it any more. You wouldn't believe the back-stabbing and politics that goes on in an office. I'm looking for a career that will provide me with a comfortable lifestyle without the pressures of corporate life. I don't want to climb the ladder of advancement. I didn't even get my foot on the first rung at Heddingtons'.'

'Your choice,' said Charles as Alex returned.

'Come to your senses yet?' said Alex.

Brian ignored the comment and continued to share with Charles. 'Everything they do is written in the church calendar. You do this on Easter Sunday and that on Easter Monday. It's straightforward. The calendar rolls over year after year.'

'But is there any money in it?' Alex entered the conversation.

'It's not only about money. What's the most expensive thing for a household these days?' Brian paused for effect.

'A mortgage, if you can afford to get into property.' Charles took the bait.

'Exactly,' said Brian. 'The church provides a house for their ministers. And that's not all. Telephone, electricity, a good salary, and superannuation.'

'If it's so good, why doesn't everyone become a minister?' Alex wanted to know.

Brian decided not to answer that one. 'According to Sally, the church calendar is sort of a manual with everything written down. What you have to say and when you have to say it. Weddings, funerals, ordinary services, special services.'

'Sounds pretty boring,' Alex reacted.

'You've got an interesting job then, have you?' Charles chimed in.

'You'll soon get used to it,' said Brian.

'What do you mean I'll soon get used to it? I'm not joining the church. You speak for yourself,' replied Alex.

'I'm just trying to share the benefits and the absence of continual confrontation with a boss. You'll virtually be your own boss,' Brian added.

They kicked this subject around during regular visits to the pub, and it became the subject of the month. In the end, Charles considered the worst thing would be that a church career would restrict his sleeping around and sharing his self-assessed excellence as the local stud. He'd exercised what he considered to be his charm for quite some time now, and he thought perhaps the time had come to settle down. He consoled himself with the thought that he wouldn't be able to settle down unless he had a stable job, and Brian's description of church had attractions. At least Brian had first-hand experience of corporate work at Heddingtons', so he knew what he was talking about. It was easy to convince Charles, but Alex was something else.

Brian's underlying theme of a church career was one in which there was no pressure or stress, everything was provided in real terms, and he didn't have to manufacture anything or be committed to production deadlines.

Alex continued his usual response to Brian's suggestion to join him and Charles in a church career.

'The joke's gone on long enough. You're still pulling my leg, aren't you?' said Alex.

Alex often had difficulty separating fact from fiction, especially when he saw the issue as something beyond his understanding. He often switched off and didn't participate in these discussions. He couldn't even remember if they'd been going on for a couple of weeks or a couple of months.

Brian had tried to guide him through the process of evaluation, but it was clearly beyond Alex.

'What's the problem?' Brian enquired. 'Do you know what the job involves?'

'Haven't got a clue,' said Alex.

'Then how can you make an informed decision if you don't know what's involved? You might even like it—you might even be good at it.' Brian tried to encourage him.

Brian was aware of Alex's limitations in dealing with issues—or rather, not dealing with issues. It was up to Brian to guide Alex through the benefits of a career in the church. Charles listened as he usually did. He'd formed his own opinions of what the job involved. Alex eventually gave in not because he could remember any of the detail but because he was easily influenced. He was able to remember the things he wanted to remember. A regular wage, no particular fixed hours, no boss, and somewhere to live. But all the finer details were lost in his mind.

'I'm happy to go along with it,' said Charles. 'Seems to tick all my boxes.'

In the end, Brian's influence had convinced Charles so that Alex's mind was made up for him.

'OK,' said Alex. 'I suppose it means I'm in as well. No argument to make. Easy come, easy go. What else am I going to do? About time someone else bought a round of beers.'

Charles decided to change the subject. 'You'll never guess who I bumped into this morning. I was having a cup of coffee—'

'Does coffee have anything to do with who you bumped into?' Alex wanted to know. 'And in any case, you said we'll never guess, so why should we try?'

Charles ignored the attack. 'Do you remember that kid at school who couldn't speak English? His name was Carlos. Well, he speaks perfect English now, but you'll never guess what he does for a living.'

'What is this, a guessing game?'

'OK,' said Charles. 'He's a Catholic priest!'

CHAPTER TEN

IN WHAT WAS becoming a parallel universe, Charles became another conquest for the dean's wife. Her sexual appetite had a tendency towards young men, perhaps because she was able to guide them towards her own fulfilment. She was widening her sexual horizon. She liked variety as well as inexperienced young men.

She exercised her seductive influence on Charles, which wasn't difficult. He was aware, as any man would be, of the attractive and seductive nature of the dean's wife. He knew the dean was overseas, and an invitation to the deanery was not to be refused, irrespective of her motive. It was a reasonable deduction, and he was more experienced than Brian. Charles probably had a similar and limited exposure to any serious sexual experience, no more engaging in quality than quantity. The dean's wife knew all men were different and wanted to explore the prospect of another quest for her sexual gratification.

His first encounter at the deanery was more direct than Brian's. She simply took his hand and led him upstairs to the bedroom. She didn't need to ask him if he would like to have sex with her. He started to take his clothes off immediately as he entered the bedroom. What else would she invite him there for, tea and scones?

Charles was the same age as Brian, which made him about half the age of the dean's wife. She explored his body in sensuous touches and firm feeling. He responded like another inexperienced lover, and she quickly grasped his level of experience. Not much, but no concern. She was going to teach him, and Charles was going to be another conquest.

When she'd first started her extramarital relationships, she would introduce them to touch and feel. She would say to them, 'There's nothing wrong with touch and feel, but you need to be gentle and caress, not grab or squeeze too hard. Here let me show you.' She would take their hand and gently place it on her breast. 'Feel the sensation you have yourself and recognise the sensation it's having on me or the girl you might be doing it with. It has to be something you both want to do as well as both enjoy. It's very important not to engage with the notion you're doing it purely for your own sexual gratification.' *Do what I tell you, not what I do myself,* she thought.

She would then show them how to gently move around the breast so as to caress the nipple in the palm of their hand.

'This is preliminary stuff,' she would explain. 'As part of the process of getting to the next stage, if there's to be a next stage. If you go straight down between my legs, you might get an immediate and negative reaction. You'll end up with nothing! If, on the other hand, you do as I'm suggesting, you'll get something at least.'

They'd all ask sensible questions in pursuit of sexual etiquette, such as 'How do I know when to move on to the next stage?'

She could see they were enjoying the initial experience, and she didn't want to rush. She was enjoying the process of encouragement too much. She was in control.

'It's all about action and reaction,' she'd say. 'If a girl shows no intent to hold back, the next step might be to see if she's prepared to take her bra off or let you take it off. If she's willing, it not only shows agreement, but also enhances the sensation of touch and feel.' She took her bra off and placed his hand back on her bare breast.

'Does it feel more sensual without the bra?' she'd say, as if she didn't know.

She could see their erections but her excitement was in the controlled knowledge of her young men's inexperience.

They were willing to learn but reticent to hold back. She was leading them, controlling them.

'What do I do next?' they would usually say in realisation she was trying to encourage.

'It would depend upon your partner's willingness to either go all the way or to engage in some sexual activity other than actual intercourse. For example, your partner may unzip your fly and feel around, in which case you have some expectation of things going a bit further. Let's experiment. What would you do if I started to do that to you?'

'Absolutely nothing,' was always the response. *Is she going to give me a handjob?* Except they didn't have to wonder for long. As she did, she would confirm there was a willingness on both parties to proceed.

At the end of what she'd considered to be a lesson, she would make the point. 'If and when any such encounter isn't going all the way, the gentleman must be prepared and able to accept the word *no*.' She elaborated by describing how difficult it would be to hold back emotionally, and it was not just the male who could get carried away, especially in the combination of two young inexperienced partners. Of course, she'd explained this from her position of experience. This whole issue was presented as being very powerful, and young men needed to be introduced to the dangers, not the least of which might be an unwanted pregnancy.

The bedroom scene progressed! One moment, she was dressed; the next, she was naked. It was always the same with younger men. They stood speechless like statues, not knowing what to do next. She undressed them, not quickly but firmly, and led them to bed.

She took the young man's hand again and showed him how to caress her thighs. 'Start at the knee, outside the right leg, and slowly stroke your way up, and you can go round the back and squeeze there quite hard. It's just muscle round the back, so you're unlikely to hurt me.'

Then she introduced caressing up the inside of her left leg. 'This is a very important area,' she said. 'If you are having an intimate relationship like this with a partner and you approach this area and she says no, you have to stop! If you don't stop, then it could be considered rape, because any further progress would be without consent. This is a very important thing to know. It's also very difficult to do. Your natural instinct will be not to stop, and this is why it is so dangerous. If there's no objection, then you continue to the top between my legs.'

Young men usually accepted these directions as guidance and tutoring, but in reality, it was the time she liked the most, holding them back from their natural instinct.

She liked to talk dirty, but it was too soon in these relationships. Her language would change as she progressed further along her process of tuition. 'Slowly caress your right hand up my inside leg, and gently put your middle finger up inside me. It should be wet and juicy.'

He was already there and didn't need to be told where to go. She was ready now, having tantalised him almost beyond his ability to withstand. This was the part she enjoyed the most. She built them up to a point of their loss of control where she had absolute control. She pulled the young man on top of her, and needing no further instruction, the young men completely lost control.

It was usually all over in a couple of seconds, as she knew it would be because it always happened that way. As the young man collapsed on top of her, she reaffirmed her previous instruction of knowing when to stop. Her little game of teach and tease was almost over.

'You will now know that when penetration is inevitable, there is no holding back. You have no control over what your body is doing.'

'Yes, yes, yes, when can we do it again?' was always the response.

The dean's wife's pleasure was in the foreplay leading up to the unique release of her young men's ejaculation. Every time she experienced it, she would think there was nothing remotely like the feeling she experienced with these young men.

She didn't want to rush things because she planned to have a number of encounters, which would bring them up to her required performance. Charles was quickly sexually satisfied and withdrew.

'How did you like it?' the dean's wife asked, seeking compliments.

'Pretty good. I'd better get going now. Lots to do.'

She escorted him to the front door. 'Would you like to come again?'

'If you like.'

They'd shared physical contact, minimal words, and mutual acceptance.

Well, that was different, she thought.

Alex was not left out of this triple encounter. However, it was much more difficult to get him to accept an invitation to the deanery. If he'd known the dean's wife had seduced Brian and Charles, he might've been more likely to respond more quickly, but Alex was Alex. She'd absolutely no idea of his difficulty in expression or response due to his ADHD. She recognised him as different, but then all men were different. Wasn't that the pleasure of her encounters?

SYDNEY JAMES

'Hello, Alex, this is the dean's wife. I'm telephoning to see if you'd like to come to the deanery this afternoon?'

Seduction never entered his mind, and why would it. His two curate friends hadn't shared their experiences. As his mind raced through possible excuses, the silence became embarrassing. Eventually, Alex responded, 'Sorry, can't this afternoon,' and he hung up. *What on earth was that all about?*

In between entertaining Brian and Charles, she tried again. 'Hello, Alex, I've got something to show you up at the deanery which I think you'll really like. Could you pop in this afternoon?'

'Sure, what time?'

'How about three thirty p.m.?'

'Okay.' And again he thought, *What's all this about?*

The dean's wife was a bit nervous trying to get Alex to bed.

I have to come up with a different plan of action for Alex. I can't gently lead him upstairs by the hand. She decided a full frontal nude approach at the front door would grab his attention, as it would also leave no doubt to her intent. As she shut the front door behind him, she presented herself in all her nakedness. He would have to get the message surely.

'How do you like this, Alex?' she said, holding her arms out to reveal all.

He got the message as his practical senses took over.

They never made it upstairs and had sex on the floor behind the front door. Alex was a bit slow in some areas, but ADHD didn't impose any restrictions under these circumstances. She was impressed by the size of his erection, stamina, and strength. He was a much more physical young man than the other two, and the variety was a welcome change.

I wonder if he's ever heard of foreplay? she thought.

He knew where he was going and didn't mess about getting there. Alex was going to be a challenge for her to have any level of control, but then she wasn't looking for uniformity.

The dean's wife had three very different sexual partners in the curates. All were the same age, but the difference in their sexual behaviour was as diverse as she could have possibly imagined. *I think I'm going to have a great deal of fun teaching these young men how to achieve a level of sexual fulfilment. Not just for them but mainly for me.*

CHAPTER ELEVEN

THE TRIPLE SEDUCTION by the dean's wife had gone according to plan—her plan! The three curates weren't the only conquests she'd made; they were just her current conquests. Such was her unconventional married life with the dean.

She'd changed the venue from the deanery to a motel for a variety of reasons, not the least of which was to maintain her privacy from gossiping neighbours. It also saved her having to clean the bathroom, wash the sheets, and numerous towels after showering.

Brian was still her favourite because of his innocence and inexperience. As a consequence, he was the most malleable. Even though he'd made several visits to the motel, his continued nervousness enabled her to excite him into embarrassment. She loved it when he became embarrassed because she could linger in seduction as she watched him try to overcome his feelings. She didn't think he felt guilty and he certainly didn't think of it as sin, but he always seemed to be somewhere else and not fully engaging. In some way she found this rather difficult to cope with, wondering if her powers of seduction were limited.

The motel was a typical two-and-a-half-star single-story with parking round the back. Each unit had a parking lot by their front door. Nobody else was there at this time of the afternoon, so he parked in the space next door. She heard his car door and footsteps on the gravel. She was waiting behind the door but waited for him to knock and kept him waiting a few moments.

'How lovely to see you again, Brian,' she would say, as if not expecting him.

Brian looked behind him to see if there was anyone around.

'Don't be embarrassed,' she would say. 'There's nobody around at this time of the day.' She loved to embarrass him—all part of her seduction. She closed the door. 'Would you like a cup of coffee or something else to drink?'

His answer was always 'No, thanks'. He just wanted to get on with it. When Brian arrived for a 'lesson' (as the dean's wife liked to think of it), he would act as if it was his first encounter. He still needed guidance, even encouragement to get on with it. He kept his clothes on, and she slowly undressed him, prolonging his embarrassment. At this stage of tuition, he was at least able to engage in some productive foreplay.

Charles's seduction was matter of fact. He'd have his clothes off almost before the motel door was closed. She was able to slow him down a bit, but he was also in need of more tuition. He was ready to withdraw when he'd climaxed and was oblivious to her needs. It was all about him. 'Well, that was nice. Thank you very much. See you next time.' She decided she would have a serious change of tuition for Charles next time he came to visit. *I'll introduce him oral sex.*

If Brian was manipulable and Charles needed to be, Alex was still uncontrollable. His appetite was nowhere near as strong as hers, but there'd been a process with all three curates. They were predictable in their repeat performances. She enjoyed Alex's immediacy as well as his stamina. He was certainly well endowed. *But I need more from these three young men.*

She often reflected on the differences between her three lovers. She liked the variety, and perhaps she was being too critical of their abilities to come up to her standard of performance. Her excitement, which had peaked at the beginning of the relationship, seemed to be going a bit off the boil.

CHAPTER TWELVE

BRIAN WAS RECALLING his leadership of his two friends into the church. On their way to the usual Saturday night's beer at the Pig and Whistle, it was raining. Brian was in smart casual clothes and had an umbrella. Charles, as usual, was overdressed and smart with a raincoat and hat. Alex was in shorts and a T-shirt totally oblivious to the rain. As soon as they were settled with their first beer, Brian announced his plan. He could remember as if it was yesterday.

'I know we've been talking about it for some time, but I've now made an absolute decision. I'm going to join the church!'

'I thought you'd already joined Sally's church.' Alex misunderstood the context.

'I thought you'd already left Heddingtons',' Charles added.

'Yes, that's right. As a career choice, Heddingtons' was a mistake, but I don't have to stay. I am able to change my mind.'

Alex caught up with the context, 'Why on earth would you leave such a well-paid job?'

'We've been talking about it for ages,' said Brian. 'Anyway, it's got nothing to do with money. If they paid me twice as much, it would still be boring and have no future.'

'Well, I think you're crazy. If I had a good job, I'd hang on to it for dear life,' said Alex.

Not if you were in my situation, thought Brian. He felt the need to justify his decision. 'You can say what you like because you've not experienced it. Anyway, I was bored to tears, and the stress was getting at me. I had no idea what I was supposed to do.'

'I thought you were supposed to be an architect,' said Alex. And that closed down the conversation until the next round of beers. This was one of the difficulties in discussion because they never seemed to go anywhere. It seemed to be talk for talk's sake, instead of moving on. It was easy to talk the talk, not so easy to walk the walk.

Alex was in his element in the pub. All the regulars greeted him. No words, just a nod or a raised finger. It said, 'I know you. I see you in here often.' The response could simply be a raised eyebrow—'Gotcha!' This was one of the reasons Alex liked it so much—because he was accepted for who he was, just a bloke having a quiet beer. No justification or confrontation, just simple acceptance. If you wanted to speak, you did; if not, you didn't. The second round of beers was on the table, and the discussion picked up again.

'So how's it going with that girlfriend of yours?' Alex wanted to know. He could have said 'The one with the funny clothes', but Alex simply said what he was thinking, so he said, 'The one with the big tits!'

'Really good,' replied Brian. 'I should get in her knickers pretty soon now.' This led Brian back to his earlier discussion.

'What I've been working on is not only a plan to get into Sally's knickers, but I think the church is the key to open her and other's doors. I don't want another dead-end job like Heddingtons' but one with security and something I can do without having a boss looking over my shoulder all the time. No Allan Jenkins hovering around. If I was to become a minister in the church, I wouldn't only have all these things, but I think it would impress Sally so much she couldn't resist. We aren't really getting anywhere other than a grope around. It's bloody frustrating when there is so much of her available.'

'I'd be happy to have a grope with her any time,' said Alex.

As usual, Charles didn't contribute to this type of discussion. It was beneath his dignity, but he did enjoy listening to his two friends bantering.

Alex decided to enter the discussion again. Apart from the fact he always felt comfortable in the pub, he loosened up verbally after a couple of beers.

'So tell me again, what's so secure about being a church minister?' said Alex.

Brian thought he knew all he needed to know, so he shared, 'It's not so much what you do as what you say. So you shouldn't say anything to contradict church doctrine. Of course, you mustn't say anything to criticise the bishop or archbishop.'

'Like what?' Alex wanted to know.

'Like making a public statement about the Bible in opposition to what everyone is supposed to believe or making a public comment about something the bishop or archbishop had said. It's a bit like a club where all the rules are written down, so you know what not to do or say. All the activities a minister leads are in a manual. I've told you before, the church calendar. Anyway, I think the time has come to stop talking about it and do something. I'm happy to give it a go and see what pans out. If nothing else, I think it will get me into Sally's knickers.'

There followed a long period of silence as they each developed their thoughts. Charles—as usual, the silent thinker—took a sip of beer. Alex downed the remaining half of his glass in a single gulp and stood up to get the next round.

As soon as Alex had gone, Charles asked, 'Are you really serious, Brian? I know we've talked about it plenty of times, but are you really serious?'

'Deadly serious!' Brian replied. 'I've burned my bridges.'

Alex returned with three beers, and as he walked towards their table, steam rose from his wet clothes as the temperature in the pub started to dry him out. It was getting busy now, as if someone had turned up the temperature as well as the volume. Maybe the alcohol loosened tongues and people talked louder, or maybe because there were more people in the pub trying to make themselves heard at the same time. Alex felt absolutely at home. He knew almost everyone in the saloon bar by sight. Nobody challenged him about where he was working, what he was wearing, or his ungainly hair. By the time he returned to the table, he'd forgotten all about the discussion about the church, he was simply into his next beer. He gently rested the glasses on beer mats already soggy, and he looked at them both.

'What?' Alex said.

'Nothing, we were just talking about Brian's plan to change jobs.'

'Oh that, I thought we'd finished that before I went for the next round.'

In fact, it wasn't spoken about any more that evening. Brian and Charles were considering their options; Alex's thoughts were elsewhere. At times like this, Alex was blissfully ignorant of life outside the Pig and Whistle.

CHAPTER THIRTEEN

WHEN BRIAN WAS living at home with his parents, the only time family got together was at meal times. 'I've decided to become a minister in the Anglican Church,' he decided to release his bombshell. *I won't mention I've actually left Heddingtons'!*

'You look serious, but are you really?' said his father. 'What do you know about religion other than what they taught you at school, which probably wasn't much?'

His father's questions were mostly considered rhetorical, so the absence of any response wasn't unusual. However, he continued. 'It's amazing how something as important as a career, perhaps for life, has attracted such little consideration.'

Without rising to the bait, Brian said, 'Charles and Alex are going to join me in theology college. They both have dead-end jobs and have agreed to try something totally different.'

This was developing into Brian's plan for the future, not just for him, but also for his two friends. Every Saturday-evening discussion at the Pig and Whistle was about the church—not so much about what Brian was doing, but more about what he'd encouraged his two friends to do.

'We're going to enrol together in theology college so we can help each other through training.' Brian was trying to steer the conversation towards a collective commitment. 'My friends are a bit nervous, but I'm sure that when we actually do it, we'll be able to support each other.'

'But none of you have the slightest idea what's involved in the church,' his father was quick to repeat.

'So we're going to find out by enrolling, then we can decide whether to continue or not.' Brian decided it should be his last word.

'So you plan to throw away a career with Heddingtons'?'

The silence that followed was not unusual for discussions to end like this in the Braithwaite household.

Charles decided to tell his parents. 'What do you think, Mum?'

'It sounds like a good idea. I wouldn't want to discourage you from such a worthy profession. What do your friends think about it?'

'They've decided to do the same, and we'll support each other during training.'

His father felt the impulse to comment. 'Alex will need a bit more than support if he's joining you. He's a square peg in a round hole, if ever I saw one.'

Alex's parents reacted in similar disbelief but were supportive. There'd been previous talk of job changes, which never eventuated because it was much easier for Alex to say what he planned to do rather than actually do it.

All parents adopted a wait-and-see attitude.

Discussion at the pub changed direction as they each became rather accustomed to Brian's proposal. Brian was anxious to get started because he was currently unemployed.

'Let's get signed in so we can find out what it's all about,' they agreed at last.

Because they'd all applied at the same time, a group interview was arranged.

Brian, at least, was aware the process was one of enrolment after interview, followed by a series of lectures and, eventually, exams to prove a level of competence. As soon as exams were mentioned, Alex reacted.

'You never told me I'd have to take exams. You know I'm no good at exams, so that counts me out.'

'We'll help you, won't we, Charles?' said Brian, trying to keep the group together. 'Let's just enter the course and see how it goes. Remember, we aren't making any commitment until we know what it's all about.' Brian always seemed to provide an escape clause but wanted to get on with it.

Charles was cool with this, but Alex still seemed to need ongoing convincing. Brian continued leading the way.

'Let's just try it and see how it goes. If it becomes too difficult, we can always bail out. Let's stop looking at the problems and focus on the benefits.'

'What benefits?' said Alex. 'You're the only one getting into Sally's knickers, and I can see that's a benefit to you. What's the benefit for me?'

'That's what we are going to find out,' replied Brian. *I'm beginning to think keeping Alex to a decision is going to be more difficult than doing the course,* thought Brian.

Charles agreed. Time for another beer and silent reflection.

The guy behind the bar thought there had been a death in the family, because they weren't their usual chatty selves who came in every Saturday evening.

'What's up, mate?' the barman enquired. 'Someone died in the family?'

'No,' said Charles.

'You look like you've lost fifty bucks and found a dollar.'

'Nothing wrong,' said Charles, and he took the beers back to his friends. He was unhappy about the whole idea, but he'd no other plans. He didn't understand the power of Brian's influence over them. He thought he'd made a choice, but he hadn't—it had been Brian's choice.

Whereas they each had their own personal feelings about the career redirection, they each had a common feeling of fear—the fear of the unknown.

CHAPTER FOURTEEN

THE GROUP INTERVIEW went rather well. The principal was a jolly man approaching (if not past) retirement age, and he seemed fascinated three young men should have a calling at the same time.

'I've never had three friends want to give their lives to the Lord at the same time. I guess this is an example of the hand of God working in a mighty and mysterious way.'

Alex had the same thought, *It sure was mysterious!*

The principal did most of the talking and encouraged them to enter campus in their ultimate service to the church. Rather than an interview where they had to convince the principal of their abilities, it was the principal trying to convince them to enrol. After the interview, they all relaxed. Enrolments completed.

'Well, that was easy,' said Alex.

'Especially since you didn't say a word,' said Charles.

'Looks like we're in then,' said Brian. 'Stage one done and dusted.'

They attended their first lecture. There were about twenty others. The lecture hall was a large auditorium with a stage at the front and wooden bench-type seats typical of church pews. The sound system worked well, and the lecturer didn't need to raise his voice. He spoke naturally, as if sharing with a group of people in close earshot.

'These seats are uncomfortable. How long is this going on for?' Alex was impatient to leave. He wasn't used to sitting still for a couple of hours.

They sat at the back of the group, which was only two rows from the front. The auditorium would've seated a couple of hundred. When the lecture ended, they drifted out together, not wanting to mix with the others.

At the end of each semester there was an exam, Brian and Charles had no difficulty, but Alex struggled. The examiners were incredibly patient with Alex, recognising something spiritual in him. They examined him in verbal discussion rather than subjecting him to written tests. Even so, Alex had found the study part of qualifying difficult, not because of the reading or the lectures but because of what he was expected to remember. At least nobody called him Master Bates any more.

'Why do I need to know all this stuff about the Holy Trinity?' Alex quizzed his two friends one day after lectures. 'What's the point of all this teaching?'

Brian tried to humour him. 'Just go through the process, listen and learn what you can. Don't give up before you've hardly started. We'll help you, and when you're employed, you won't need to remember it anyway.'

A great deal of the study was sitting in a lecture hall, which Alex found incredibly difficult. He fidgeted all the time, wanting to leave and go to the pub. Brian and Charles always made notes. That was fine because they always shared them with Alex.

Alex felt the need to ask a deep and meaningful. 'Why do they stand up there and lecture us from their notes so we can take notes? Wouldn't it be easier and quicker for the lecturer to just give us his notes? It would save a lot of time and effort. Save us sitting around listening to lectures.'

'Just relax, Alex. Go to sleep if you like. Charles and I are taking notes, and as usual, we'll share them with you,' said Brian.

Eventually they each became curates/assistant ministers in the church. Alex, who could be so easily described as totally unmotivated in any career prospects, took to it like a duck to water. He'd gravitated towards Brian at school because he was always able to obtain support for his every need. Neither Brian nor Alex realised even yet that they both needed each other for opposite reasons.

Brian continued to lead and encourage. Charles quietly went along for the ride. Alex, on the other hand, wanted to be in the shadows, unseen, non-confrontational in anything. He always accepted Brian's advice as being the right answer because if he'd looked at an alternative, he would have been confused and unable to choose. Much better to just have one opinion and accept Brian's advice. Brian became Alex's protector and advisor. Neither had realised Alex was afflicted with attention deficit hyperactive disorder (ADHD), and his lifestyle had been influenced by his inability to foresee the consequences of his decisions or actions.

Brian's realisation didn't change their relationship, but it did motivate him to learn about ADHD by searching the Internet. He learnt the effects were a difficulty focusing on any single issue. Multiple issues were impossible. Those who suffer found it impossible to sit still, even for short periods. Most people didn't understand these behavioural issues, which were sometimes extreme. Symptoms created a major impact on the daily lives of those afflicted as well as their immediate family and friends. The more Brian learnt, the more he understood his friend Alex.

When Alex had left school at sixteen, he'd got a job with McDonald's and moved around the hospitality industry, changing jobs for a few extra dollars. He was a typical spotty-faced teenager eating the wrong fatty food, drinking the wrong sugar-filled drinks. He would leave a job in preference to addressing a simple issue like his irregular time-keeping.

This had no effect upon Alex's career ambitions because he didn't have any. Provided he'd enough money to buy a few beers at the weekend and occasionally go to the movies, he'd no desire for anything more grandiose. He spent little to no money on clothing or shoes, and his very limited wardrobe gave the impression of him almost being a street person. He could see no point in buying a new pair of shorts for $180 when he could buy a perfectly good pair at St Vincent's or some other op shop for $5. Maybe this was a psychological hand-me-down from his childhood, like hand-me-down clothes he always had to wear from his older brothers.

They were in the Pig and Whistle one day, and Charles made comment about Alex's dress sense. 'You're wearing the same T-shirt and shorts you wore last Saturday.'

'So?' said Alex. 'Is that a problem?'

'No, I'm just saying because I've changed my clothes every day since.'

Alex took a long draw on his beer while he thought of what to say.

He didn't take kindly to criticism, even from Charles. He put his glass down, got up, and walked out of the pub.

'What did I say?' Charles wondered. 'I only suggested he changed his clothes a bit more often.'

'He doesn't think about clothes like we do,' Brian said authoritatively. 'It's not as if he can't afford them, he just doesn't like shopping. If he went out now to buy new clothes, he would probably buy a pair of shorts and a shirt exactly the same as he's wearing at the moment.'

'I don't understand him or his attitude towards clothes and people,' said Charles. 'He's a good-looking bloke and could pick up any number of girls if he spent a bit more time on his appearance. He always looks like he needs a haircut and rarely shaves.'

Brian measured his response. 'Even if we could get him to wear attractive clothes and pick up a girl, he wouldn't know what to say or do. He couldn't cope with the prospect of rejection. It's all too confronting for him. Life is too confronting for him. You'll never change him, and if you try, he'll just get up and walk away, like he did just then. He can't deal with confrontation.'

Unlike his two friends, Alex didn't wonder what he might be doing in five or ten years' time. He just lived moment by moment, day by day. Alex had no other interests apart from alcohol. The more obvious—girls were mostly beyond his reach. There was nothing lacking in his libido, and he'd developed a good physique. But one day was much the same as the last for Alex. *Wasn't it the same for everyone?* he thought. *Everyone just lives for the weekends, don't they?*

Alex returned to meet his friends at the Pig and Whistle the following week as if nothing had happened. He wasn't one to hold a grudge. More likely, he'd forgotten about his altercation with Charles.

Charles tried again to help Alex. 'So what do you do when you see a girl you fancy or she makes eye contact with you, Alex?'

'I look the other way', said Alex, 'because I don't know how to take the next step.'

'Just go up to her and say, "Hi, my name's Alex. Are you here on your own?"'

'I tried that once,' said Alex. 'She said she was there with her boyfriend, so I looked a complete idiot. I've never tried it again.'

'You'll get a few knock-backs, but it's no reason give up. You just have to keep at it.'

Between beers, Charles spoke to Brian about the insecurity surrounding everything Alex tried to do, although it wasn't as if he tried to do very much. Brian decided not to share his knowledge of ADHD with Charles. It gave him a degree of superiority in his responses to Charles's. Brian just accepted Alex couldn't change. He was who he was. There were girls who wanted to fulfil their own needs and desires with Alex, but eventually there came a need for communication and Alex couldn't cope. The effect of any social interaction fed Alex's insecurity. The girls thought he was playing hard to get, so they tried harder. Occasionally, they succeeded.

After they'd been deaconed, they continued to meet at the Pig and Whistle for a quiet beer on a Saturday evening. They daren't walk into the bar wearing a dog collar. None of them could have kept a straight face in the sure response all the occupants would think they were dressed up for a fancy dress party.

CHAPTER FIFTEEN

THE DEAN'S CAREER path in the Anglican Church had been one of natural progression, since his parents were churchgoers and he'd grown up attending church regularly. During this period, anyone who attended church was considered to be Christian. It was a Sunday activity, distinct from the rest of the week when they were as secular as anyone else. So the dean had been a churchgoer because his parents were churchgoers!

'The church is changing,' the dean explained to Brian. 'When I was a kid, we did as we were told. We accepted our parents knew what was best for our future career. You are living in a different age, having been encouraged to consider your own future.'

Brian felt the need to comment. 'My father had things to say about my career path and was much more supportive of my employment with Heddingtons'.'

'Did he agree with your decision to leave Heddington's and join the church?'

'No, of course not.' Brian had to agree.

'For me,' the dean continued, 'it was the only career my parents considered, and I can't recall having made any contribution to the decision to become a minister. My advances through the church were similarly unplanned. A job was on offer in administration and they appointed me. Nowadays the system has to be officially advertised and applicants are interviewed by committee.'

'I think they call it transparency,' said Brian.

'Whatever you want to call it,' responded the dean, 'it's different now.

'That brings me to share something with you, Brian. You've had exposure to the world outside the church, and I've been impressed with your presentation. You can command attention addressing an audience. I'd like you to consider a career in the church of high office. Notwithstanding what you refer to as transparency, I have influence and can make things happen. Anyway, at this stage, I would like you to consider the opportunity, and we'll talk about it more when I return from my overseas trip.'

There were many young men wanting to become parish priests and have active ministry. There were a lesser number who had more professional aspirations, and the dean was one of these. He sought positions in the church other than ministerial, such as accountancy, business management, teaching, and lecturing. He was also an acceptable author not only of homilies but also books of an apologetic nature about religion.

'I don't really consider myself a clergyman, Brian, but of course, I was ordained and can celebrate Holy Rites.'

When he was a single man, the dean attended many overseas study groups, enabling him to have stopovers in South East Asia. Rest and relaxation facilitated his hidden passion. Stopovers were more normal in those days. Airlines needed to land more frequently to refuel, and they provided overnight accommodation in a city hotel. At these times, he was able to become someone else. Far from home, his stopovers developed into two or three nights. It had no financial impact on the church because airline tickets were all-inclusive of stopover hotels. Neither the church nor the airline cared if a passenger stopped over for an extra day. Hotels in the region were cheap, so the dean willingly paid the extra hotel accommodation out of his own pocket if he stayed an extra night.

He was attracted to street life in cafés and bars as they sprung up after dark. He became aroused as he remembered walking the city streets, admiring the colour of young women's clothing and the oriental smell of cooking. He noticed the freedom with which people sat down and chatted over coffee or beer. He'd no sooner sat down at a street bar when a very attractive young lady sat down with him and smiled. She looked like a teenager; she was so young.

'Would you like to buy me a drink?' she said.

It seemed the natural thing to do, and because he was away from home, he knew there was no chance of being recognised. He responded positively with a smile and a gesture of the hand. She spoke very good

English as small talk drifted around other clients as they sat and chatted. He'd started with a coffee, but because she was drinking champagne, he changed to beer. When he felt he'd had enough to drink, he thanked her, and she withdrew in a very courteous manner. She bowed and moved backwards, never turning her back on him.

He'd gone to the bar to settle up. This was unusual because at home every drink had to be paid for before consumption. However, here the barman kept a tab, and customers settled up at the end.

'How much?' he asked the barman.

'Two,' was the reply.

'Two what?' said the dean.

'Two thousand baht,' said the barman.

He remembered his reaction at the cost of drinks. He thought he'd been taken for a ride, and as he walked back to his hotel, he decided he'd never do it again—two thousand baht! He couldn't wait to get back to his hotel and use his calculator to find out what the cost was in US dollars. He was reasonably familiar with the value of US currency. He checked the calculation several times. It had actually cost him US $56, or $28 each. Four drinks each, $7 a pop.

I think I'll do it again after all. It was incredibly cheap.

He'd never been particularly attracted to women sexually, although he was able to engage in outward relationships verbally, which would otherwise be considered heterosexual. This behaviour enabled him to happily engage with these young girls on the street cafés and bars.

CHAPTER SIXTEEN

DURING THE DEAN'S formative years as a young man, he'd been interested in amateur dramatics and discovered many people in theatre had a similar leaning towards alternative sexual inclinations. This didn't make him feel outcast. Quite the contrary, it made him feel comfortable. However, he was unable to have any serious relationships with heterosexual women who were unable to recognise his tendencies.

His memory of theatre was a combination of sensual experiences and inclusion. The producer welcomed him. 'Hello, young man, I do hope you'll love being part of our acting family.' It wasn't simply a handshake; it was an embrace which lingered. 'Come and meet the gang. We have such a mixture of talent here.'

They were in the middle of rehearsals, and the gang were dressed up and wearing heavy make-up. Overlaid with the scent of greasepaint, the smell of old clothes having been in mothballs for years infiltrated his nostrils. The theatre had its own smell of aging props and worn carpet. It had clearly seen better days, but none of the cast seemed to notice the decay. They were part of it!

'This is our leading lady, Eileen. It's not his real name!' This was confusing because she appeared to be feminine. 'His chosen surname is Dover. Get it? Eileen Dover!'

They were all laughing, but he was yet to get the joke.

'Let's try another,' said the producer. 'This couple are of Scottish heritage. We call her Ben and her chosen surname is Doon. Her partner is Phil McAffity. Get it? Ben Doon and Phil McAffity. It's just a bit of fun as we become different people when we perform.'

As he met more of the cast, he became more comfortable. It would be an interesting challenge to become someone else, even for a short time. They were all very tactile towards him, and he was on the receiving end of many hugs, embraces, and kisses.

His drama experience awakened a natural ability as an orator as well as an actor. It gave him confidence as a speaker long before he entered the church. He'd learnt how to gain attention from an audience. He could say something, pause, and look around his audience, as they were attentive—even eager—to hear what he would say next. Many orators would speak continuously in monotone. He'd learnt to pause. Even a long silence became more effective as he confidently surveyed his audience. He would bring this skill with him into the church and was teaching Brian its use and benefit.

The dean's overseas lecturing tours provided the opportunity to develop his acting ability, not for the purpose of performance but to become someone else. His first attempt had developed during a walk one evening after dinner. He'd left his hotel and followed the lights and the sound of music in an area devoid of any such goings-on during the day. The smell of Asian cooking out in the open was seductive. He'd just had dinner, but his nostrils searched for recognition. Some he knew, others he didn't.

I love this experience. It's like being in the theatre. I don't know a soul, and nobody knows me. I could be anyone I'd like.

He was drawn towards a street café with a few empty tables. *I'll have a quiet beer and watch people as they meet and interact.* Although he was sexually attracted more towards men than women, he wouldn't have described himself as homosexual. He was just diverse in terms of his deepest thoughts and desires. As a young man, these desires went nowhere; but as he developed, he found fulfilment in the world of transsexuals. He was attracted towards what outwardly appeared to be young women but who were, in fact, young men overdressed and over-made-up. He was excited by the street negotiations for a night out and could enjoy this type of company with absolutely no restrictions. It made him feel free from the restraint set upon him at home by the church and society. In any case, this type of entertainment wasn't available at home.

He'd had a few unconventional experiences with these overdressed young women/men, but his excitement was aroused more from the completely open verbal encounters than in the physical relationships.

This changed during one of his overseas trips, when his deepest sexual persona was awakened.

His appetite for unique sexual gratification grew as his trips to overseas seminars became more frequent. It became a natural step from his deanery persona to the other persona in whom he felt more comfortable. As he stepped off the aeroplane, he divested himself of his clerical persona and entered his natural persona. The reverse was true when he went back home, shedding his true self to the respectability the church expected of him.

On subsequent trips overseas, he gravitated naturally into street life. Again, as soon as he sat down, a young person joined him with the usual question, 'Would you like to buy me a drink?'

He went straight into a beer and started to chat with his guest. 'What do you do for a living?'

'Anything you like,' was the response. 'Would you like to come back to my place and find out? My name is Georgie.'

The dean saw no point in sharing his real name, and in any case, his guest wasn't interested. He thought of Eileen Dover and chuckled to himself. Things had moved beyond a level of verbal communication. They left their table, he paid the bar tab and followed his escort round the corner to his place of 'work'. As the youngster undressed, the dean was impressed by his body—its slenderness and smooth, consistent colour. The aroma was one of spice, not perfume, and it aroused his curiosity as his first oriental sex was on the verge of fulfilment.

The dean was getting older now and things were changing. Transsexuals no longer satisfied him, as the need for control influenced his developing persona. He became more interested in young boys who were just as available in the stopover region of his choice. It was this aspect of control and power that became the motivation for his ultimate sexual gratification. Well, it always had been, but fulfilment was a process achieved through experience and defined by his ongoing needs. Of course, he wasn't alone in these desires, and a number of men travelled the same journey to indulge in their choice of sexual transgression.

CHAPTER SEVENTEEN

ANOTHER DEVELOPMENT WAS taking place in the dean's character. He was becoming jealous of his wife's freedom created by his own action of travelling overseas.

The dean's wife noticed a change in his character, and it had come to boiling point shortly after he'd come home from his last trip.

'I want to talk to you about what you get up to while I'm away,' he said.

'What on earth do you mean?' She'd never been challenged so directly, and the dean was standing over her in a menacing way.

'I've given you some sexual leniency, but I want to make it clear that if you bring my position as dean into disrepute as a consequence of your extramarital activity, I shall deal with you in the most serious way.'

She daren't ask nor did she want to know what he might do, so she held her counsel.

'Do I make myself clear?' the dean emphasised, shouting in her face.

She could think of nothing to say other than yes in the hope it would end the confrontation. She wondered what'd brought that on and decided to talk to Brian about it. She'd never been scared of the dean before; there'd been no reason. He'd changed noticeably, and she was afraid.

Apart from their honeymoon, which had been disastrous sexually, there had been no subsequent physical contact between them. It had never been put into words, but the dean had turned a blind eye to her sexual needs without really knowing the extent.

She'd never been afraid of the dean, but this experience had changed the relationship. She wondered how she was now going to manage her sexual deviations. *Brian will know.*

She drove the dean to the airport for his next trip with his parting words. 'Don't forget what I told you, or you'll be sorry!'

On the way home, she called Brian, and they met discreetly in a road lay-by. They sat in the car, and she offloaded her fear. The only thing Brian could suggest was to discontinue their relationship.

'Don't you think that's a bit drastic?' she said.

'I don't know how serious the dean's threat might be. He hasn't told you he knows about us, has he?' Brian tried to give comfort, but it was the only thing he could think of saying.

'What scared me most was the look in his eyes, and he's never spoken to me like that before. I'm sure he's not jealous of me having sex, especially as he doesn't want it himself—at least not with me. He's much more concerned someone might find out and make it public. Then he would be involved in a scandal. I believe he could be very cruel in preference to having his name at the centre of a gutter press story.'

'We'll have to be very careful in the future then,' said Brian.

They were unable to suggest a solution and parted sharing their fear. Brian was fearful of his cushy job and the prospect of a career path to high office in the church. She was in fear of fear, because she didn't know what to do to alleviate her fear.

CHAPTER EIGHTEEN

THE POSITION OF dean had been offered at the right time— he was the only qualified applicant. Apart from his theological qualification, he also had a business degree in management. As dean of the diocese based at the cathedral, he didn't have parish duties, although he was expected to present the occasional sermon. He was very good at sermons and able to give direction on any issue supported with biblical chapter and verse, both Old and New Testament. However, his knowledge was entirely cerebral, and his understanding of biblical narrative was of the secular world. He was able to produce sermons incredibly quickly because he'd mastered cut and paste from the Internet.

When he'd been offered the position of dean, his parents were delighted.

'Well done, son,' his father had said. 'You've done us proud.'

His response was silence as they were seated in the parlour of their semi-detached home in the suburbs. The parlour was the traditional room in the house, set apart for Sunday. There was no TV or radio in the room, and the furniture was utilitarian. He remembered the décor because it had never changed throughout his childhood. His father's minimal words of encouragement were not as etched in his memory as the drab wallpaper curling up at the bottom. The worn arms on the settee suite and the virtually threadbare carpet, which in those days wasn't wall to wall but had a gap around the edge, created additional housework for his mother. The net curtain prevented anyone from looking in, and they never had visitors. The musty smell was in his nostrils every time he thought about the parlour.

His mum gave him a hug and a kiss. 'Well done, darling.' Such physical contact was rare.

He often reflected on that day, having reached the pinnacle of his career and yet his parents seemed to consider it nothing particularly special. He'd been a loner at school and university, and it suddenly impacted upon him, he'd also been a loner at home.

It was his ideal job for a variety of reasons. One being he was at the top of the diocesan tree and didn't have up-line management accountability. Even though the cathedral was the seat of the dean with responsibility for diocesan spiritual guidance, the only up-line managerial was the archbishop. The dean's principal responsibility was administrative.

He did have to deal with chapter members, but they were a committee of elders to which the word *age* was more relevant than *belief*. The dean was a master at manipulating committees, and it was bread and butter to him. The chapter was supposed to be an association of clerics and laity forming a moral body of spiritual opinion instituted by ecclesiastical authority. The purpose was intended for the promotion of divine worship as well as to assist the bishop in governance of his diocese. However it had declined into a committee of aged and vested-interest men, who influenced their conservative belief in order to prevent change.

Young ministers with spiritual enlightenment entered the church with great expectations to change things for the benefit of the church. But the old school elder's chapter quickly quenched any spiritual ambitions. They were also cerebral in belief. They knew best because they'd known it longer than anyone else.

On a broader scale, a situation had festered in some parishes regarding the issue of renewal. The chapter was required to give guidance, and so a meeting was convened.

'Gentlemen,' said the dean, 'we only have one item of the agenda, to give guidance to our parishes how to respond to what appears to be a groundswell movement. They want more freedom to witness the ministry of the Holy Spirit. They call it renewal.'

'What do they expect us to say?' asked one member.

Another said, 'What do they want to renew?'

The meeting continued for about an hour, during which time two elders dozed off, and the discussion never got to the issue of what renewal really meant. It was thought to be giving freedom to exercise something they hadn't done before.

'That can't be right,' said one who was awake. 'If it hasn't been done before, whatever *it* was, then it can't be renewed, can it?'

'We can't allow parishes to do what they think is best,' said another member. 'It will fall apart, and there will be no discipline.'

'Can't allow what?' said another who suddenly rose from his slumber.

'Tell them no, they can't change. Tell them to read the Thirty-Nine Articles of Religion. We can't have one or two parishes going off on their own doctrinal way. Doctrine is doctrine. Always has been, always will be. It doesn't need renewal.'

'Let's put it to the vote then,' said the dean. 'All those in favour of leaving things as they are, say aye. Those against? I think the ayes have it. Motion carried. Thank you for coming, gentlemen. Sorry to keep you up so late.'

The dean had no interest in Christian ethics and could preach as well as anyone, probably better, except these were versions of his overseas presentations. It was easy for him to tell other people what to do or how to lead their lives, especially when he could support his argument with biblical narrative.

He would've liked to have acquired an accountancy qualification but never felt comfortable with balance sheets, profit-and-loss statements, or even financial statements. He could do arithmetic, he was competent at adding columns of figures, but fitting them into the accounts to reflect shareholders' financial interest was beyond his ability. He was much happier dealing with people; he could control them!

He enjoyed management, which for him meant the selection and control of subordinates to achieve a plan. This was a major influence in his sexual persona in the area of control. His managerial directive was broadly Christian because of the environment in which he worked. However, he always had a hidden agenda, which he enjoyed keeping to himself. This part of his character provided the excitement of clandestine manipulation of staff. He knew what he was doing and why he was doing it, but those he employed didn't need to know.

The dean reflected on a series of meetings he'd had with a minister in his diocese. The Revd Owen Jones, tall and lanky—a slow thinker, even slower speaker. He would make appointments to meet the dean and share information. Owen thought the arrangement was reciprocal, except it took him quite a while to figure out he was being used as a source of parish information and getting nothing in return.

'My dear Owen, how lovely to see you again. What's going on out there in your parish?'

'Thank you, dean. We've many challenges, especially in the order of service from the Book of Common Prayer. We would like freedom to worship as the people want, instead of being locked into First Order or the Second Order. Also the language needs bringing up to date.'

'Very commendable, Owen, but we have to recognise these things should not be changed at the whim of one parish.'

The dean could have told him he was already working with a committee discussing this very issue and a draft would be released shortly from his office. The fact that it was a good idea was suppressed with Owen. *Can't let the diocese think it was Owen's idea. When it gets released, everyone will know it was my idea.*

Because Owen was a slow thinker and the exchange of ideas was only a couple of times a year, it was a few years before he worked out he never got any information from the dean. He stopped his visits.

The dean wouldn't have described himself as a control freak, but very few people were aware of their own idiosyncrasies. It was much more natural for the dean to see other people's faults than his own—an altogether human failure.

He continually worked on his style of management that kept everyone in the dark about his objectives. Much easier to get each member to do their part and save time in meetings, argument, and debate.

CHAPTER NINETEEN

A NOTHER STRATEGY THE dean shared with Brian was to convene a meeting and introduce a contentious issue for discussion. This wouldn't represent his opinion, and it didn't matter what the issue was. The intent was to get emotion, even anger, into the discussion, during which he would remain silent. He would listen and let them discuss uncontrolled without making verbal judgement about opinions voiced.

'It's a good way to get people to open up and learn what they really think, Brian, instead of what they say they think,' the dean explained. 'Listen and learn at the staff meeting this afternoon.'

All staff members were invited, including the dean's secretary and the verger. As the chairman, the dean opened the meeting. 'I had an email from a member of our congregation enquiring about the Holy Spirit. He wanted to know how and when we receive a blessing from the Holy Spirit.'

The dean could have asked their opinion, but there was no need. His senior minister took the bait. 'We receive a blessing from the Holy Spirit when we're baptised. That's the first blessing. The second blessing is at confirmation. What else is there to know?'

The dean's secretary attended a different parish church as well as the cathedral, and this lit her fuse. 'Is that what the Bible says, or what you say?' she replied with some venom in her voice.

The verger wanted to say something, but his junior position restrained him. The dean recognised this. 'You have something to say, verger? The whole point of our staff meetings is to say what we want to say in the confidence of this room. So let's hear your opinion.'

The verger was unable to escape a response. 'I thought the Holy Spirit was a person who we could call upon at any time for spiritual guidance. We can receive a blessing several times if we invite the Holy Spirit into our life.'

'Absolute rubbish,' said the senior minister. 'You're either Christian or you're not. A woman can't be half-pregnant, she either is or she isn't! If you've been baptised and confirmed, that's all you need to know about the Holy Spirit.'

After the meeting, in the confidence of the dean's office, Brian was asked, 'What did you think of the meeting?'

Brian needed clarification. 'What do you mean, about the Holy Spirit or the reactions?'

'About getting a reaction from people who don't normally contribute, or others who would be restrained in a response,' said the dean.

Brian was cautious. 'Well, it seemed to work. I had no idea the senior minister was so passionate about the issue.'

'That's the whole point. You do now, and that's the benefit of my strategy. There's no way I would have got him to declare his belief by asking him in private. He would have told me what he thought I wanted him to say. By the same token, the verger would have said nothing.'

The dean's trips overseas would follow a similar secret agenda. Clearly he didn't want anyone to know what he did during stopovers, it was nothing to do with anyone else. His marriage wasn't one he'd anticipated, but they'd both got on well together because both needed to be accepted by society, despite their sexually diverse idiosyncrasies. Neither was looking for a partner, let alone marriage, but a common purpose was fulfilled in their relationship.

They were secretive with each other about their own needs and desires. The dean's wife wanted a relationship more than a little out of the ordinary. She was actively heterosexual and had no expectations of finding a man with anything like her appetite. So she'd chosen the dean who'd give her the appearance of respectability while leaving her free to roam sexually outside the relationship. It also suited his purpose, although she had no idea why.

Neither was aware of any details of each other's desires or needs. The dean's wife only knew the sexually inept husband who lived at home; she had no idea what he got up to overseas. But he didn't know what she got up to while he was away, so this qualified the mutually acceptable relationship. Any discussions they had were domestic. Things unsaid were kept confidential.

Whenever the dean returned home, an open and truthful relationship would've been ridiculous. So dialogue always followed a less-than-honest discourse.

'Did you have a good trip overseas, dear?' she might say to open friendly discussion.

'Yes, thank you, my dear. The usual discomfort, of course, in travelling overseas with customs, immigration, and security.'

'And how about your speaking engagements?' She didn't really want to know, but this was the type of discussion they'd often have, nothing truthful or honest.

'How was your time while I was away then, dear, anything important?'

'Not really. I've been showing Brian around, developing an appetite for high office on the ecclesiastical ladder. He seems pretty keen to learn.'

And so the dean and his wife presented a relationship to each other much the same as they did to the church and society, being one of matrimonial normality, whereas in reality it was one of convenience, secrecy, and abnormality.

CHAPTER TWENTY

THE REACQUAINTANCE OF Carlos was considered unusual only for the reason he'd become a priest. He was ignorant of the reasons his school friends had chosen a church career.

'At least you can speak English now,' said Alex as a typical insensitive comment.

They all laughed. Discussion questioned Carlos's reasons for taking up orders. He was too discreet to enquire the reasons his three friends had taken to the cloth.

'You must come and join us for a drink at our local,' invited Charles.

'Better still, come to my church and let me offer you some Catholic hospitality.'

'Is it free?' Another of Alex's insensitive remarks.

Brian and Charles were used to Alex putting his foot in his mouth, but Carlos knew nothing of his characteristics other than school-day memories.

Fr Carlos Resendez was assistant minister at St Mary's Mother of Jesus. His senior minister was involved in land acquisition for the purpose of building a retirement village. Carlos rarely saw him and conducted services without supervision.

'So what happened to you when you left school, Carlos?' Brian wanted to know.

'I travelled overseas, particularly around Greece and Turkey. My family thought it would help me decide on a career, which they suggested in the priesthood. My mother's background is Irish Catholic, and my father is Spanish.

'Help yourselves to a drink.' Carlos decided self-service was appropriate.

Brian and Charles each had a short spirit with ice, and Alex a whiskey with no ice in a tumbler. *Well, I might only get one,* thought Alex.

Carlos shared an idea. 'Why don't we meet here once a month and discuss theological issues in private? It would give us a platform from which to learn about the hidden differences between Catholicism and Anglicanism.'

Alex thought that was a good idea, but then he had an ulterior motive. Given their total absence of spiritual involvement, Brian and Charles weren't so keen.

CHAPTER TWENTY-ONE

T HE DEAN CONDUCTED a service of Holy Communion following his return from overseas. The diocese was always pleased to see him again. He never considered his overseas activities as extramarital because he didn't have a marital relationship. In part, this enabled him to justify his activities, and he'd absolutely no intent of trying to justify them to anyone—certainly not to his wife.

Unlike the Catholic confession, which is spoken in the first person— 'Father, I have sinned'—the Anglican church and all its derivatives speak collectively: 'We have sinned against you in thought word and deed. . . . Father, forgive us.'

As directed by the Book of Common Prayer, the dean would say, 'This is intended to administer to all who shall be devoutly disposed the most comforting sacrament of the body and blood of Christ, to be received by them in remembrance of his meritorious cross and passion, by which alone we obtain remission of our sins and are made partakers of the kingdom of heaven.'

The purpose of administering this holy rite was to exercise forgiveness for the transgressions of the congregation. He never thought he needed forgiveness; he was totally divorced from the other person who took over during his overseas trips. He would lead them in prayer known as the General Confession, except this was not for him to say. It was for them to say, in order for him to administer absolution. The congregation would say together, 'Almighty God, Father of our Lord Jesus Christ, maker of all things, judge of all men, we acknowledge with shame the sins we have committed, by thought, word, and deed, against your divine majesty, provoking most justly your wrath and indignation against us. We earnestly repent and are heartily sorry for all our misdoing. Have mercy on us, most merciful Father. For your Son, our Lord Jesus Christ's sake, forgive us all that is past and grant us that from this time forward we may serve and please you in newness of life, to the honour and glory of your name, through Jesus Christ, our Lord. Amen.'

The dean always felt righteous when he was able to forgive others (on God's behalf) all those who were taking part in this service as he was able to pronounce absolution for them!

'Almighty God, our heavenly Father, who of his great mercy has promised forgiveness of sins to all who with hearty repentance and true faith turn to him—have mercy on you [not himself], pardon and deliver you from all your sins, confirm and strengthen you in all goodness, and keep you in eternal life, through Jesus Christ, our Lord. Amen.'

This was a major failing in church teaching—Catholic as well as Anglican, and its many derivatives—because in the Bible, the operative word qualifying forgiveness is *repentance*. The dean displayed complete ignorance for this requirement to turn away from and not repeat his transgression or sin. Others in the church hierarchy seemed similarly unaware of this, as did some congregational members of other denominations. The dean's fallen human nature enabled him to justify absolution as meaningful for those he led in Holy Communion. His knowledge of biblical truth never touched his lifestyle. In any case, his transgressive behaviour only happened overseas, so judgement was not an issue.

CHAPTER TWENTY-TWO

As EXPECTED BRIAN, Charles, and Alex had been appointed a parish curacy and fell into the routine of doing tasks delegated by their senior minister.

'I thought we were going to be our own boss,' complained Alex when next they met at the pub in mufti. He'd forgotten all about the transition of being a curate before being appointed a senior minister in charge of a parish. Brian explained it to Alex again, but his memory only lasted as long as the beer in his hand.

Most clergymen looked very presentable in a plain blue shirt and white dog collar, but Alex was able look a bit shabby. He didn't notice it himself. He used a laundromat for washing his clothes, and everything went in the bag-wash. The first day of wear, his clothes were clean and reasonably tidy; but by the second day, they looked shabby again—probably because he still bought his shirts and trousers second-hand from the op shop.

Brian had a special introduction to his congregation by the incumbent senior minister.

'Let me introduce you to our new assistant minister, Revd Brian Braithwaite, who's had experience outside the church. He used to be a successful architect but sacrificed a very lucrative and successful career with Heddington, Heddington, and Boswell to devote his life in service to the church.'

Without exception, every congregation member (including the senior minister) unquestionably believed this story. Heddington's reputation was all that was necessary to elevate him retrospectively in his sacrificial persona. Without even trying, his pride took a step heavenwards.

Brian continued to struggle to make progress with Sally, and his frustration was continually challenged when they kissed and she put the brakes on. Then one day, 'Would you like to come round to my parents' house this evening,' she asked. 'We could have a quiet evening together. My parents have gone away for the weekend.'

Her parents' house was perfect in every detail—furniture and marble-top kitchen bench, geometric garden with painted concrete gnomes guarding every corner. It didn't display any homely character and seemed to be on display for imminent sale. He felt uncomfortable, but if this was his opportunity to get into Sally's knickers, he could put up with it. He was hopeful but not optimistic because she'd previously been able to stop any serious progress.

When he arrived, there was a pleasant smell of food—she'd ordered Thai takeaway!

After some petting, she set out the meal and they fed each other. First a prawn delicately placed in his mouth. Then he'd stabbed a piece of tofu with his chopsticks and offered it to her. She was much more adept at chopsticks. It didn't matter, the process continued with interludes of wine.

They never finished the meal or the wine, and Sally took him to bed.

She wore a white lace negligee, no knickers! *Very virginal,* thought Brian. He wondered, If they'd been married, would this have been their honeymoon night? It certainly played out that way. As a consequence, a hasty wedding had to be arranged because in nine months, there was to be an addition to Sally and Brian's new family. Apart from the obvious, the urgency of an official wedding was justified by the dean's expectation that clergy comply with the institution of marriage. Procreation in wedlock was to be the cornerstone of any minister's fulfilment in God's plan and purpose.

They'd been provided with a lovely little house close to the church. He got everything he'd expected apart from a car, but there was a pool car he could use if he needed to visit anyone in hospital or other pastoral duty.

The dean continued his special interest in Brian, perhaps because he'd given up such a lucrative and promising career as an architect. Brian's friends convinced him he was being singled out for high office. He was invited to meetings about finance, how to get on to boards of directors and trust companies, making friends with the media so when public comment was required, the media knew whom to ask. Brian was a very presentable and well-spoken individual and had no difficulty standing in front of a group and holding their attention as he spoke words reflecting the dean's agenda. The same confidence helped him in front of a camera, and he was just as comfortable in a TV studio as he was in the pulpit or at the lectern. He made special efforts to associate with people who were publicly well known, celebrities or politicians. TV and radio personalities, authors, and newspaper editors were also in his social circle. These were not friends but people whom he could call upon for his needs of personal exposure.

He found it useful to introduce himself to a new group in a similar manner to his original church introduction. He didn't need to mention Heddingtons, and it was sufficient to say he'd come into ministry as a mature person, having had experience outside the church. In other words, he'd not come straight from the seminary with no experience of life. He was a worldly man. This always appeared to be well received, but he never realised that in his immaturity, he was overdoing these introductions. Those who heard it made appropriate comment beyond his earshot and, in Christian love, said he would doubtless grow out of his sinful pride.

CHAPTER TWENTY-THREE

BRIAN'S ENTRY INTO the church had nothing to do with sacrificing a successful career in architecture; it had everything to do with drifting into what he thought would be an easy and non-challenging lifestyle. But could he perform the role to the acceptance of his peers, his superiors, and his congregations? Well, he had so far.

In her way, Sally had fulfilled her plan and purpose having selected Brian for his DNA. In any event, their feelings were mutual, and they fell into what was commonly accepted as marital normality. It was now time for Sally to change her style of dress, and the mismatch of clothing and colours disappeared overnight; Brian didn't notice a thing. Before long there was another baby; and for Sally, the perfect family—a boy and a girl, Nicholas and Georgina.

A sensitive situation developed when they were both awake and early to bed. Brian remembered the white negligée he hadn't seen since the night they spent together in Sally's parent's home.

'Do you love me?' Sally asked.

Funny question, thought Brian. 'Yes, of course, I love you, darling, it's why I married you.'

'But you never tell me you love me, so I'm just asking.'

This had happened a number of times, and Sally seemed to need reinforcement of the words, which Brian disassociated with sex. He wondered if this was leading somewhere, especially since he'd become more experienced in his sexual activity with the dean's wife.

He made an effort to change the subject. 'Why don't you come on top of me and try it a different way?' Brian tried to engage her with his experience.

'No, that's not the way to make love. Why are you suggesting we do it differently?' Sally was a lovely girl but was somewhat limited in fulfilling Brian's developing sexual desires, having had absolutely no previous experience, so the honeymoon period was fairly short-lived.

'I saved myself for you and never made love with anyone else. My parents told me this was very important for a Christian.'

'But sex is supposed to be enjoyed as well as to have kids.'

'I agree,' she said. 'But I'm talking about making love to each other, not having sex!'

Sally turned over, sending the message that sex was not on the menu tonight and the discussion was over.

Brian hadn't been searching for any other sexual activity, and he thought rejection happened in marriage after children had arrived. Since he was still able to reflect upon his earlier stressful life as an architect, marriage, like ministry, became comfortably acceptable.

He was aware the dean's wife had, at the very least, massaged a growing interest in his sexual appetite. He was yet to understand the feminine gender and was experiencing two extremes of female sexual desire. With Sally, it was an act of love, which may or may not result in procreation. With the dean's wife, it was not love but purely sex, with no other possible outcome apart from physical satisfaction.

The dean's wife never asked him if he loved her. *An altogether irrelevant question,* he thought. Sally was becoming more sensitive about Brian's love for her, and he was becoming more demanding of Sally's sex as a direct consequence of his tutorials with the dean's wife. Sally developed a fear of loss of love, except it was in her own mind as an expectation of marriage. Brian hadn't lost anything yet.

CHAPTER TWENTY-FOUR

IT WASN'T LONG before Alex's senior minister took issue about his style of ministry.

'You're attracting the wrong type of people into my church. They're predominantly fringe people. Some are homeless, even druggies and alcoholics. You have to understand, Alex, they don't contribute anything!'

They certainly were people with a very low self-esteem, usually suffering from deep depression. Whatever the reason, their attire usually gave them away. The senior minister's only concern was they were takers not givers.

'They're unable to contribute to church life,' he went on to say. 'They don't only fail to contribute to offertories but don't take part in any church group meetings. They only come when there's food around.'

Alex didn't recognise the distinction, but after it had been brought to his attention, he could see what had previously been obvious to everyone else. At morning coffee after the service of Holy Communion, the congregation moved into the church hall. It was austere in as much as the chairs were uncomfortable and trestle tables with paper table cloths. Coffee was instant with cold milk, and people stood with intent to make a hasty retreat. Tables were spread with sandwiches and cakes. Alex's people stood together on one side of the hall, tucking into the food. Nobody else could get near. Instead the 'normal' congregation stood back, making uncharitable remarks about their unwelcome guests.

'Anyone would think they'd never had anything to eat. Just look at them gorging themselves. There'll be nothing left for us.'

They discussed the matter with their senior minister. 'You'll have to do something about this, Reverend. It's not only they eat all the food, but they smell. Don't they ever take a shower?'

The senior minister was aware many people lived on the streets without a home, but instead of enlightening his congregation, he bowed to people pressure to get rid of them. Even though he knew it was un-Christian, he complied with the populist view.

On the other side of the room, Alex and his group were aware there was discussion about them, and one said to Alex. 'Don't those people want anything to eat. There's loads of food here?'

'Perhaps they're aware we have no homes or income and are happy for us to have a good feed. After all, it is a church, so they're showing Christian love,' said another.

Alex could see himself in all these people. He was able to engage with them easily without judgement. He reached out to them, spoke to them, and encouraged them to come to church not for any spiritual reason but simply because it was his generous nature. He was offering them something that nobody else would—friendship, love, purpose, and fellowship. Alex wasn't like this because he'd attended seminary; he wasn't taught this. It was his natural self, the way he lived and moved and had his being.

Alex was aware that more often than not, they responded because the invitation offered a warm place to sit, have a hot drink, and a sandwich, which might be the only meal they had all day. Word got around quickly in the parish, and it wasn't long before the 'fringe' people outnumbered the 'normal' people in the congregation, and this was the senior minister's gripe.

The fringe people became Alex's downfall as well as his destiny because his bishop thought he would be ideal to take a senior minister position in a parish filled with people having this misfortune. An inner-city suburb with a decrepit old church building needed to be used by the church was just waiting for someone like Alex.

Like his friends Brian and Charles, he'd entered the church for all the wrong reasons and had little understanding of 'churchianity', let alone Christianity, but Alex believed there was a God. He'd simply not learnt how to understand God during his theological education. Little did he know this was a very general problem for many clerics. There was no doubt it was a problem for Brian and Charles.

Theology had been all about learning biblical narrative, and he'd absolutely no training on how to deal with these people gravitating towards him. Nonetheless here he was, exercising ministry in its truest sense, having fellowship with the unlovely. A more Christian act would be difficult to imagine as he gathered his flock around him.

His appointment as senior minister solved two problems for the church. It moved the undesirables away from Alex's curacy church, as well as utilising an empty inner-city church. On this occasion, there was no need for Brian's intervention or the archbishop's assistance.

There was no churchwarden or church council. Alex was on his own. All of a sudden, he was his own boss. Alex had yet to learn about church hypocrisy of labelling people between the haves and the have-nots, which ultimately affected people's self-esteem. He didn't realise that in many respects, he was a have-not himself!

Because the church building was old, cold, and unwelcoming, Alex decided to conduct his services in the church hall. The heating was much more effective because the building was more modern, having a low ceiling instead of the vaulted ceiling in the church, where all the heat disappeared through the roof.

At the end of the service, he made an announcement. 'Dear friends, I invite you all to stay after the service. I've made some lovely hot soup. It's ready, but please organise yourselves some tables and chairs, and make yourselves comfortable in the warm.' They didn't need much encouragement.

As he opened the kitchen door, the smell of the soup attracted everyone to stay. Who wouldn't stay for hot soup?

As his congregation grew, his largest saucepan had to be replaced with a cauldron.

'If you grab a spoon and a bowl at the end of the table and help yourself to a bread roll and come down to the end, where I'll ladle out some soup.'

They were the most orderly crowd, no pushing or impatience, so grateful to get a hot meal and sit down in the warm with others of their kind.

It was a simple but wholesome meal, and many said they'd never had such good soup. Alex ate the same meal with his guests. During the meal, he circulated and listened to people and spoke words they thought were prayers. Alex didn't realise he was simply having fellowship with his congregation, something they thought unique in the church or anywhere else for that matter. Clerics had never spoken to them before!

'So how was your day?' Alex enquired as he sat down next to a lady to eat his soup.

'Much the same as usual, except I've been looking forward to this all day.'

Alex was delighted, saying, 'I'm so glad you're enjoying it.'

'It will set me up for when I get out on the street to find somewhere to sleep.'

Alex had no idea how to pray. It was another thing they never taught him at seminary. His limited exposure to prayer was hearing clergy quoting scriptural passages from memory. He couldn't remember any, so he convinced himself he didn't know how to pray. He became aware of it one day as he was speaking to one of his homeless people. Another overheard him having fellowship and asked, 'Would you please come and pray for me when you have finished praying for him, Reverend?'

They loved to call him Reverend, and he loved it too. It gave him a feeling of self-worth, something he'd never experienced before.

Brian thought he was helping Alex deal with ADHD when he said, 'I realise you're trying to help your street people, but don't you think they're becoming dependent on you?'

'Of course not. Where else are they going to get a meal?'

'But do you have to do it every day?' Brian tried to steer him away from it becoming a burden. 'You could do your soup thing once a week and something easier like sandwiches another day. You're making a rod for your own back. These things will add up to the cost—electricity, cleaning.'

It was too much for Alex to cope with. He was no longer concerned about what soup to make, he was now worried about the electricity bill. ADHD was like this; he could only focus on the last issue Brian spoke about.

Alex could never remember the collective substance of these discussions and could only handle one issue at a time. His attention span prevented him from storing things in his mind for later recall, in which one issue had influence on another. This always fuelled his insecurity, leading to depression. His solution was found in the spirit—not yet the Holy Spirit but Johnnie Walker or Jack Daniel's spirit. A few shots weren't enough to deaden the emotional pain; it usually needed half a bottle just to get him through the day.

Outwardly he was seen to be coping, and nobody had any idea what he was going through or how he self-medicated with ever-increasing dosages of the spirit. He never appeared to be drunk because he was able to hold his spirit without it affecting his balance or speech. In fact, everyone—including his congregation and especially his bishop—thought he was achieving wonderful ministry. The truth however, was he could only do it with the help of Johnnie or Jack.

Occasionally, things got too much for him. The need for half a bottle became a full bottle, following which he crashed and spent a couple of days in bed, unable to minister. His housekeeper Alice was the only one who knew the truth, because she threw away the empty bottles. She also covered for him by making excuses he would be unavailable for ministry for a few days. She became his enabler with little white lies about the state of his health. He eventually rose from his bed and got back to work and people saw him as if recovering from illness, looking drawn and haggard. He always vowed never to do it again because he felt so wretched on the downside of the binge. But the spirit was always stronger than his ability to abstain. Easy to say, not so easy to do.

Eventually Alice tried to help. 'Don't you think you should try and do something about your drinking problem, Alex?'

'It's not a problem. I can give it up any time I like.'

'Then why don't you?'

'Because I like having a drink. There's nothing wrong with liking a drink.'

'I agree,' said Alice. 'I like a drink occasionally, but it's getting a bit out of hand when you get through a whole bottle of whiskey and more in a day. It can't be good for your liver. Have you tried Alcoholics Anonymous?'

'Yes, of course, I have, and they're absolutely useless. You sit around in a circle and share each other's problems. I don't want to hear their problems any more than they want to hear mine. They call it therapy, but it drives me to drink. So just leave it, OK?'

'I'm really trying to help you, Alex. Your periods of sobriety have a repetitive cycle of about six months. Each time, you say you'll never do it again. Can't you remember the pain you put yourself through last time?'

'I don't expect you to understand, Alice. I don't understand it myself!'

It needled him inch by inch back down the path of self-destruction.

Alice tried a different approach. 'How about I make an appointment with our local doctor? He should have some suggestions.'

Alex wasn't impressed, but he was desperate and reluctantly agreed. The doctor was a mature man of Indian extraction having a mannerism of head shaking horizontally. Alex found this unnerving and found himself trying to copy the movement involuntarily.

The doctor took pulse rate and blood pressure, looked in his ears and eyes, stuck a cold stethoscope over his chest. Alex was impatiently losing confidence. *What's all this got to do with my difficulty?*

Then doctor's first words: 'What is your difficulty, Mr Bates?'

As usual, Alex was lost for a meaningful response. After a long silence of head rocking, Alex said, 'I don't know if you can help.'

It quickly became apparent the doctor had no idea because he didn't consider Alex's condition to be a disease. His professional opinion was that it was an issue of self-control—to drink or not to drink.

Alex went back home and didn't bother trying to explain to Alice. What was the point?

Alice was tidying up and doing some housework.

'What have you done with my Book of Common Prayer? I left in on top of the TV.'

'I put it on bookshelf with all your other books,' she told him.

'In the future, please don't hide my things away. I know exactly where everything is, so it would be really helpful if you don't move my stuff!'

She understood him better than he understood himself, so she was never upset by the occasional outburst. He always apologised later, and she was able to build up a deep understanding of his character, including his faults, which weren't limited to alcohol. She was a good Christian, aware nobody was perfect. When confronted by Alex's faults, she would always bring to mind the Bible's advice. *Don't look for the splinter in Alex's eye. Look for the log in your own!*

CHAPTER TWENTY-FIVE

CHARLES SETTLED INTO his curacy without difficulty. His senior minister had been in service with the same parish for twenty-five years and was close to retirement. It was more common for senior ministers to move around from parish to parish, usually after two or three years. The effect of his senior minister's longevity influenced Charles as he fell into step with routine. It was almost as if Charles was approaching retirement himself. Neither he nor his senior minister engaged in anything new or challenging.

In Charles's previous employ, instead of planning, he'd always dreamed ahead of anything his ability could fulfil. His career ambitions were as achievable as a kid wanting to be a train-driver or a fireman. He'd fantasised himself a bank manager or CEO of a large multinational corporation, whether to have a BMW or Mercedes. Deep down, he knew his limitations, and his current position enabled him to come to terms with reality. No more pipe dreams.

He remembered his father asking about job prospects.

'How's the job-hunting going?' his dad asked at dinner one evening.

'Pretty good, I've got three prospects in the pipeline, and one of them is with the bank.'

'What's the job then? Money market, corporate, or retail?'

'I don't know until I get to interview.'

'How can you apply for a job without knowing what you're applying for? Are you missing a cog in your brain?'

Whenever issues got to a point of an unanswerable question, a long silence lingered and the subject drifted into cyberspace.

Mum came to the rescue. 'I've baked your favourite dessert, Charles, bread-and-butter pudding.'

'Thanks, Mum.'

It wasn't as if Charles was incapable, but his life before ministry had been a perpetual dream influenced by glossy magazines, films, and media exposure. He'd even lived his dream to some extent, swanning around wine bars and yuppie city hotel bars where the drinks were at least twice the price of regular pubs. This was his hunting ground for what mostly motivated him, his libido! He'd a natural and engaging personality towards the opposite sex, and his reputation preceded him, most of which originated from stories he'd circulated himself. The girls he attracted were always from the same mould. Alex would describe them as 'Barbie dolls'. It was all about the chemistry of sex appeal.

It was with extreme surprise to his parents and girlfriends past and present, when Charles announced his intent to join Brian and Alex at the seminary to become a priest.

He remembered attending his first seminary experience with Brian and Alex.

'In the name of the Father and of the Son and of the Holy Spirit,' to which most responded, 'Amen.'

'Dear Lord, we gather here today in humble praise and thanksgiving. We seek your will as we share in matters concerning our future as we enter the church to serve. Guide us in the words to speak, and bless us as we use our hearts and ears to listen. Through Jesus Christ, our Lord.' Again most of them responded, 'Amen.'

'Gentlemen, this will be an informal meeting to give you the opportunity of asking questions as an introduction for entry into the seminary. Our college has been here for almost a hundred years, and most entries qualify and take up positions in the church. These are not limited to ordained priests, and there are several other career paths available such as accountancy, pastoral care, and chaplaincy. So let's get informal and hear your questions.'

Everyone was as silent as the threesome. Nobody had the courage to be first to speak, so the lecturer prattled on a bit longer, and eventually someone asked a question. 'How long will it be before we qualify and take up a position as senior minister?'

The lecturer looked around the table, studying the absence of interest, and eventually responded.

'That's a good question, but of course, it depends how quickly you learn. Generally, it takes three years. This is followed by a period of curacy as an assistant minister. It can be a year or two, again dependent upon how you develop.'

One guy asked, 'Do we earn a salary as a curate? I've got a wife and baby to support.' He seemed very nervous about asking a money question.

'A current minister's salary is $61,855 per annum,' the lecturer was pleased to announce.

Alex started to cough as his nervous system reacted involuntarily. He currently earned $700 a week and was doing the math on a piece of paper, when Brian leaned over and wrote, '$36,400 is what you currently earn a year.' Alex stopped coughing.

'Are there any meals and accommodation provided?' asked another.

'Yes, we have our own campus, mostly funded by grants—which you can apply for,' replied the lecturer. 'Sometimes your parish church will sponsor you.'

CHAPTER TWENTY-SIX

T HEY'D ALL BEEN accepted as entrants and progressed through theological training. There never seemed to be any absolute answer to questions about divinity, and when such issues were discussed, it made everyone withdraw into silence. These questions were to be resolved in prayer.

During their training, the principal, Stewart Kennedy, needed to speak to the archbishop with concerns about the threesome. There had always been a close relationship between the theology college principal and the archbishop—the principal was often appointed archbishop. There seemed to be no good reason for this other than it had occurred on previous occasions.

'Your Grace, I seek your guidance regarding three of our students in this semester.'

'Yes, of course, Stewart. What are your concerns?'

'I'm having great difficulty in relating to three particular inmates. They're clearly very close friends, but I can't imagine why. They have a relationship with each other, but nobody else. It would be difficult to imagine three young men so different in every way imaginable. One is tall and lean, another is neither one nor the other, and the third is short and stocky. One is clean-shaven, another shaves sometimes, and the third never shaves and has untidy long hair. During sessions of teaching or lectures, they always sit together. Nothing wrong with that, but others mix and sit in different places from session to session. Only one of them speaks, another seems to listen but says nothing, and the third looks as if he's waiting for a bus.'

'Stewart, I really can't see what you're getting at. They're three different students in Christ. What has their appearance or behaviour have to do with their ability to become ministers of the church?'

'It's not just their appearance. They don't seem to have any understanding of what it means to be a Christian, let alone a minister.'

The archbishop thought for several moments and eventually said, 'My dear Stewart, I do believe you're being judgemental. Your job is to teach and nurture these students into leaders of the church. Just do your job, and the leave the outcome to God.'

'Thank you, Your Grace, for your words of wisdom.' But inwardly, Stewart was humiliated, having been corrected. He wasn't confident the appointment from principal to archbishop would occur again in his lifetime. This wasn't the first time he'd been corrected by the archbishop, and he believed it wouldn't be forgotten at the next synod meeting.

Notwithstanding, all three were able to get through these sessions by listening and either agreeing with the others or massaging an earlier answer into their own words. They confined their deep and meaningful discussions in the confidence of their own company. The problem was that it became the blind leading the blind. To them, the stories they studied in scripture were just that—stories. They convinced themselves it had nothing to do with living today, which they hung on to as their real world.

Quite early in their studies, they'd come up against what had been referred to as creation, suggesting God had created all things, visible and invisible—or as the Bible put it, 'seen and not seen'. A suggestion they considered much more acceptable was that God hadn't created man; man had created God! This seemed to satisfy their humanistic or mythological understanding of all things divine. It also appealed to their humanity in the absence of anything spiritual. Alex had his doubts however.

They were living in the real world and others in the seminary were living in cuckoo land. Brian often reflected on his thoughts when he'd worked at Heddingtons. *Just stick with it, and remember the stress of eventually having to produce something. I would never have mastered the technology of CADCAM. I would never have made any progress up the ladder everyone else was clambering. I'm so glad to be out of it. I've escaped from having to produce something. I feel really comfortable where I am. I wonder whatever happened to the structural detail Allan Jenkins wanted?*

Charles sailed through theological lectures, taking notes, which he shared with Alex and Brian. They'd supported each other to ordination. They all went through the process and became deacons, ultimately taking up positions as assistant ministers. Fortunately, they were all in the same diocese, and they met frequently to compare experiences. They continued to support each other, never daring to consult with their senior minister and certainly not their bishop. In any event, they didn't really have a line of accountability to the bishop because their senior minister was, in effect, their up-line manager.

CHAPTER TWENTY-SEVEN

DESPITE HIS MANY skills, Brian was absolutely hopeless at time management. He was always late for appointments or meetings and had no conscience about keeping people waiting or even missing an appointment altogether. This included Sally. As a consequence of his ever-growing ego, he considered himself an important person. People had to fit into his busy schedule, not the other way round.

Alex was having the church calendar inflicted upon him, as were his two friends, and he tried to share problems of issues involved.

Charles's reaction was, 'If you share your problems with me, I'll share my problems with you.' They all agreed not to go there. But as usual, Alex was unable to let it go.

'Things are getting a bit out of hand at my church. Not only do I have to get up early to fit everything in, I can't even relax in the evening because of meetings.'

Brian had no difficulty with this since he was up early anyway and the day just drifted away till he got home in the evening, whatever time that might be. Church life simply controlled him, and it wasn't until the day's commitments ended that he accepted his working day had ended.

'But surely there is no other job having so many things planned for every day of the week, every week of the year. Why can't we just tear up the church calendar and do what we like? There's so much structure to everything. What to wear, what to say, where to go, when to do it. We even have a secretary to run our lives. You never told me about that, Brian, when I agreed to come along your career path.'

'Stop complaining and look at the all the good things you've got,' was all he got back from Brian.

There was a lot to do, and the senior minister was passing on the jobs he didn't want to do himself. One of the time-consuming things were funerals, and these were often long affairs during which family and friends wanted to speak to a congregation about their great loss. It became apparent to Alex that the deceased never did anything wrong in their lives and were all paragons of virtue. Alex reflected upon this as he sat at the front of the church by the coffin during a funeral service, as a procession of relatives came to the lectern speaking about family history. He wondered why none of the deceased ever came to church and yet they all wanted to have a church funeral. His thoughts were not in any way inclined towards the Christian belief of life after death. His thoughts were simply about coming to the church building.

As he was sitting by the coffin, the wife of the deceased came to the lectern to speak. 'We are saddened by the loss of our dearly departed. A good husband, father to all my children, loving brother . . .'

What a load of cobblers. She never spoke kindly of him when he was alive. He wasn't a good husband or a good father and gambled the housekeeping away.

She went on for about twenty minutes, and then the grown-up children spoke through their tears of upset. They'd made copious notes, and as each page was turned, people started yawning and dozing off.

These periods of quietness, when all he had to do was sit in attendance, gave him comfort in thinking that when he died, even though his indiscretions may be known by then, nobody would share them at his funeral.

Funerals were not only growing in number, but so did the required meetings with the family before and after the funeral service. He found himself being the minister responsible for funerals and the senior minister responsible for baptisms, a much more sociable and enjoyable rite. Baptisms never had the same congregational involvement as a funeral. A time could be set to start, and it was all over in less than an hour. A funeral could go on for three or four hours!

Charles's agenda was the same, but he'd accepted the junior minister got less favourable jobs in the parish. *In a couple of years, I'll have my own parish, and I'll delegate funerals to my curate/assistant minister.*

The threesome still met regularly at the Pig and Whistle, although the subject of the dean's wife was no longer mentioned. One such occasion, Alex was worried because he'd been on notice from his senior minister to lead a group on the biblical subject of faith. Brian, of course, had the answer.

'If anyone really wants to know, refer them to the Bible—Hebrews, Chapter 11, Verse 1, which gives a very good definition of what faith is supposed to be. "Now faith is the substance of things hoped for, the evidence of things not seen,"' Brian could recite from memory.

Alex remembered this was a difficult subject, and he'd been guided by Brian never to raise the matter other than to speak the word without engaging in any dialogue about what it might mean.

'"In the name of the Father and of the Son and of the Holy Spirit,"' said Brian. 'They're just words. Don't get hung up on what they might mean. If anyone asks, just tell him or her it's one of the mysteries of Christianity and we're not supposed to understand everything—just believe. Anyway, these words mean different things to different people, and the Holy Spirit is another of those issues we should avoid discussing.'

Brian would often remind his friends, 'You don't have to believe what you say, just say what you believe.' This was how he overcame many biblical issues too difficult to understand and guided his friends to do likewise.

It so happened a seminar was to be presented on the subject of faith, and the three curates decided they'd better attend. It wasn't so much they wanted to attend; they needed to be seen to attend as part of their curate training. They weren't planning to ask any questions on this delicate subject, just listen and maybe learn something.

The seminar presenter was a theologian of high status, having a doctorate of theology—a PhD, no less. It was expected that he would know more about faith than anyone and even how to use it. There was a preseminar cocktail function, during which wives were invited. However few wives were interested beyond the cocktails, and none planned to sit through the seminar. Brian was the only one married at this stage, and Sally was already wishing she hadn't come.

'This is what it's like darling, when you think I'm out enjoying myself.' *Please try and remember this when you complain I stay out late and you expect me to be home,* he thought.

The three curates and Sally suddenly found themselves standing next to the seminar presenter, and introductions were expected.

'Good evening, Professor, my name is Revd Brian Braithwaite, and this is my wife Sally.'

'Pleased to meet you, Brian. Please call me Roger. This is my partner, Henrietta,' said the professor in a nonchalant manner.

There followed an uncomfortable silence, and eventually Roger explained, 'My wife and I separated, and Henrietta has moved in with me now. Much more convenient and cost effective than running two homes.'

Henrietta was not in the least embarrassed, and this arrangement seemed quite normal for her and him.

Well, that maybe very liberal, thought Brian. *But isn't the professor doing what I'm doing with dean's wife, except Henrietta has simply moved in as a matter of convenience?* Did that make any difference? Not to Brian, so he didn't worry about it.

The issue of the professor's partner was another example of how the church imposed marriage upon their congregations but had a different set of rules for themselves. The same thing applied to divorce. All three curates held the professor in very high esteem for no reason other than he was a professor of theology. *He must know something,* they thought.

There was no dialogue from Charles or Alex with either the professor or his partner. There was no common ground—especially none on the issue of marriage or faith for that matter. They drifted apart, and the professor and Henrietta moved on to another set of introductions.

The seminar got under way with the usual introduction of the professor's career, which was all about the exams he had passed, the letters after his name, and the books he'd written. He was a prolific writer and critic to the Christian news media, occasionally getting exposure in the secular press. He'd never been exposed to the church other than in books and had never been a parish priest.

Eventually he was able to speak for himself. 'Well, gentlemen, we all have faith. So how much have you got? How much has the guy sitting next to you got?'

Having never been in ministry, he was an academic and could

clearly speak for hours about any biblical subject. Although these were rhetorical questions at this stage, the three curates feared they might become open for discussion. The professor continued.

'The Bible refers to our faith as being something we all need more of, because the Bible records this very fact. Jesus's disciples asked him how they could increase their faith. So I've spent my entire career searching the Bible and other books, trying to find out how we can do this.' He referred to Luke 17, Verse 5, in which the apostles asked Jesus to increase their faith, so this was the biblical foundation on which he made his case, as a doctor of theology. However, it was a question, not an answer. Brian, at least, pondered whether there would be any answers or were these all going to be questions.

He went on for a couple of hours rambling from this to that and back again. Brian thought he could have done better himself. Alex went to sleep, and Charles was so disinterested he began reading a book. It didn't matter. They'd attended the seminar and would've been noticed by whoever noticed these things.

The seminar livened up a bit during question time. 'What are we supposed to use our faith for?' one young minister asked.

Brian's ears pricked up. *Maybe an answer at last.*

'Well, to some extent it depends whether you're an Anglican or any of its derivatives, like United, Methodist, Baptist Apostolic, et cetera, or whether you're Catholic, Orthodox, Lutheran, and so on,' the professor responded.

What a load of waffle, thought Brian. *Since we're all Anglican here, what difference does it make to all those who aren't?*

There were then a series of questions bordering on the same subject.

At last, one young brave soul asked, 'What do you use your faith for, sir?'

Brian had been challenged with this question himself.

'That's a very personal question and isn't for public discussion. What I use my faith for is between me and God—nobody else,' the professor replied somewhat conclusively.

Brilliant, thought Brian. *I must remember that because it discourages* any further discussion, either on what faith is, how much we need to have, or what we are supposed to use it for.

Then the professor decided to slightly extend his answer in line with his biblical knowledge. 'Of course, I use it for my salvation,' he added.

Yes, thought Brian, *anything else? Like what use is it when we're alive, or do we just wait till we die?*

Other questions were answered in a similar indefinable manner, making Brian attentive. Almost irrespective of the question, it was dealt with in a similar way.

'That's another of those mysteries of religion,' continued the professor. 'We aren't supposed to understand everything, just believe. I'm not saying this, the Bible says Jesus said this.'

Brian had heard most of it before. He at least, came away from the seminar rejuvenated—not on the subject of faith, since he was no more informed than he'd been before. However, he was informed on how to answer those difficult questions parishioners sometimes asked. He considered the seminar had been worthwhile. His learning curve for dealing with issues increased in a positive direction, as he thought of the things he learnt:

> *Answer a question with a question.*
> *Don't believe what you say, just say what you believe.*
> *For issues too difficult to answer, fall back on 'The mysteries of religion aren't supposed to be understood. God is beyond our understanding. Just believe. I'm not saying this—the Bible said, Jesus said it.'*

He was yet to learn how to deal with telephone calls and letters, either hard copy or email. He learnt the answers by eavesdropping on some senior ministers during a comfort break.

One of them said, 'I just ignore them for a month or so. If they write again, I get my secretary to write a short reply thanking them for their letter and implying the matter is being considered.'

'What do you do then?' another enquired.

'I ignore it again. Usually it's the last I hear of it.'

'Of course, there are some who'll never let go and will eventually approach me after a service. They might say they'd written a couple of times and apart from an acknowledgement from my secretary they'd received no response. I then politely tell them I have hundreds of letters, and theirs must have slipped through the net and become lost.'

'OK, but what do you do then?'

'I pass it over to my assistant minister.' They all laughed.

There followed a period of quiet and almost relaxing ministry, during which the three curates settled down to their routine of funerals, fetes, evening groups and the occasional Sunday service sermon.

CHAPTER TWENTY-EIGHT

B RIAN'S INFLUENCE CONTINUED to cement his friendship with Charles and Alex. They didn't discuss their friendship except they each held to the expectation of continuance, for no reason other than it had been there as long as they could remember.

Their years of study became a further bonding fraternity during which they were challenged in a belief they'd never heard of. Their understanding of Bible narrative was the Christmas and Easter stories they'd often heard as kids, it bored them to tears.

Sally was the only person who'd ever asked Brian what he thought of church. Earlier in their relationship, when Brian had attended church with her as a layman, she'd asked, 'What did you think of the sermon today?'

'I didn't really understand it,' said Brian. 'It sounded plausible, but what was the message supposed to be about?'

'It was all about loving your neighbour as yourself,' said Sally. 'Haven't you heard the story of the Good Samaritan?'

'No, I can't remember any stories about the Bible other than those we heard at school. I could never understand why the Bible referred to Easter Friday as Good Friday. What's good about crucifying someone?'

'Well, you know something,' said Sally. 'Even though you think you know nothing. You know Jesus was crucified and it happened on a Friday. The good news is, three days later He rose again. So there's a bit more you've learnt.'

Brian's thoughts often flashed back to Heddingtons, where he'd learnt absolutely nothing. He wondered what use learning Jesus rose from the dead three days later was likely to be of any benefit to him. *I suppose I could learn this stuff and speak from the pulpit. It would just a speaking job.* But his thoughts were more about the benefits of a job in the church, which at that stage he saw as greener grass on the other side, not to mention Sally's knickers!

If his plan succeeded, he and his two friends would be teaching the same old stories. The wider perspective of Christianity was beyond their grasp. The responsibility for this was to those who'd taught them at the seminary. None of them were prepared or able to be creative in ministry but they'd convinced themselves they'd nothing to offer an industrial or commercial employer anyway.

CHAPTER TWENTY-NINE

THE DEAN'S COVERT selection of Brian for high office gathered momentum during his curacy. Clearly, it had nothing to do with what Brian believed in a Christian sense, it had to do with how the dean could use him. He'd recognised Brian's speaking skills, his presentation, and the way he could command attention when addressing a group of people and hold their attention, as well as influence them.

Shortly after ordination, the dean called Brian in for a chat. This had actually been Brian's first visit to the deanery, and he couldn't help being impressed at the lavish style and quality of their home. The thought never occurred to him it was owned by the church. The dean's wife opened the door, and he'd been stunned at how attractive she was. She looked so young compared with the dean. She offered her hand to greet him, invited him in and called the dean. While she did this she continued to hold his hand, which made him feel uncomfortable in a rather pleasurable way.

'Thank you for coming along, Brian. Would you like some tea or coffee?'

The dean's wife stood waiting for his response, but he was admiring her every feature instead of accepting the invitation of refreshment. He snapped into a nervous 'Thank you', so she had to say again, 'Tea or coffee?'

'Oh sorry, coffee, thank you. Milk, no sugar.'

The dean was used to men admiring his wife, and a delay often followed a first introduction. When she'd gone to the kitchen, the dean asked a few domestic questions as small talk so as not to get into anything deep and meaningful before his wife returned with refreshments. When she'd departed, he said, 'I've been following your public speaking attributes, Brian, and wonder if you've had any training, such as Toastmasters or any other public speaker tuition?'

'No,' replied Brian, 'I guess it's a natural thing, I've never given it a thought, other than I enjoy doing it.'

'I'd like you to enrol in Toastmasters. It will set you up in good stead for the rest of your public speaking life.'

'Sure,' Brian agreed. *Why not?*

The dean continued, 'I'd also like to get you involved in a few committees I currently chair. Initially I want you to listen and learn, so I don't want you to speak. I'll introduce you as an observer and, of course, a clergyman. The point is, these meetings need to fulfil a sense of involvement for attendees. They like to feel the church cares and is involved in what they are doing. I have an agenda, which I don't necessarily share with other committee members. I want you to notice how I introduce a subject, allow some discussion, make my position known, and then call for a vote. As the majority of committee members are laity, they respect my position as dean almost to the point of never disagreeing with anything I suggest. You might think I'm being manipulative, but it's in the best interests of the church. I want you to learn there are printed agenda as well as hidden agenda. This is how we get things done in the church.'

The dean was aware of the threesome's relationship because they were all invited to the deanery for the occasional function. It also made the grooming process of Brian less obvious to observers in the church who may have otherwise thought the dean's actions were giving favour to Brian. However, it was entirely clear to everyone in the church hierarchy as well as everyone at lower levels of ministry that grooming was taking place. It wasn't generally understood, however, the degree of mind-bending or secret induction that went into the process. It was all done behind closed doors, without any checks or balances. It would fulfil the dean's objectives, and that was all there was to it.

Brian enrolled at Toastmasters as directed. He didn't attend as a clergyman and was simply introduced as Brian Braithwaite. Nobody else gave any background information either, so he felt comfortable in keeping his own employment confidential.

The leader concluded introductions and invited the first person to speak. 'I want you each to stand and speak for four minutes on any subject of your choice. I will make comments at the end of each presentation. The idea is for you to overcome any embarrassment of speaking publicly, and since none of you know anyone around the table, this is as public as we can make it to start with.'

The first guy stood up to speak and unfolded a sheet of paper.

'No,' said the leader. 'You're not to refer to notes. You have to speak from memory. Any subject you like.'

This completely threw the first contender, and he hummed and coughed and kept repeating himself. He lasted about one minute and then sat down.

'Very good for a first attempt,' said the leader. 'You have to do some work on your thoughts and what you want to say. You can prepare by making notes but the point of Toastmasters is to get you on your feet and speak from the heart. Brian, why don't you have a go?'

Brian hadn't made any plans on what he would speak about. *I could speak about how I got into Sally's knickers or how I seduced the dean's wife. Or how I got myself and two friends into church careers with absolutely no Christian understanding because we couldn't survive in the corporate world.* But he chose a subject without any serious undertones.

He took off his watch and placed it on the table in front of him for everyone to see. He then looked confidently around the table and eyeballed each person, as much as to say, 'This is how you do it.'

'I want to tell you how to eat a meat pie at a football match.' Everybody cracked up laughing. 'This might appear to be very simple, but in fact, it requires a great deal of skill and only comes with experience.' He went on for his four minutes and had them all in stitches, including the leader.

'It's very important to know that gravy can be very hot and runny, so if you lift your arms up when a goal is scored, you'll have gravy running down to your elbow. There would likely be several occasions to stand up, raise your hands, and cheer—the last thing you want to do is drop your pie or, worst of all, drip gravy down the neck of the guy in front of you. You need to make small bites so as not to burn your mouth, and regular tilting the pie backwards to contain the meat and gravy has to be considered as the game progresses.'

He occasionally glanced at his watch without making it obvious, combining this look as he scrolled his eyes around everyone seated at the table.

As the second hand on his watch came up to the four minutes, he smiled a confident smile to everyone and sat down to a round of applause. He glowed with pride at his achievement. He was a born orator, and the leader suggested he had no need to come again unless he wanted to entertain them.

Unwittingly, Brian used every opportunity to feed his ego. In reality it wasn't only defined in his relationship with Alex, but also Charles and now in this totally different way, at Toastmasters. Of course, his ego was also fuelled in his relationship with the dean's wife, not to mention the church. The size of his ego gave him a sense of value and self-worth. It set him apart from Alex as well as Charles, although to a lesser extent.

There were many differences between the three curates in dress, character, behaviour, and presentation. But there was one quality they shared in equal proportion: they all had the same measure of youthful lust.

CHAPTER THIRTY

D URING ONE OF Alex's early sexual encounters at the deanery, he'd been in bed with the dean's wife when the telephone rang, and she'd left the bedroom to take the call downstairs. Alex snooped around at arm's length and opened the bedside cabinet drawer, revealing a little blue book. He was stunned to find his name on the first page, A for *Alex*. It recorded the number of times he'd had sex with her, and it froze his mind and body in fear. Before turning the page, he was happy to see several crosses next to his name. *Had it been that many times, or was this some sort of rating system she entered to record his performance?* His first reaction was to get out of bed and escape, but he was unable to deal with confrontation; his thoughts were all about what he'd say to her as he left. He could still hear her talking downstairs, and he turned the page and found Brian was there too, on page B. He quickly flipped the page again and saw Charles's name on page C.

What the hell am I going to do? he thought. But his indecision slowed him down to inaction, and he could hear her coming back upstairs. He just managed to return the book before she came back into the bedroom. She wanted to have sex again, and Alex was relieved from having to say anything. His bodily functions took over as he performed again in silence.

CHAPTER THIRTY-ONE

THEY WEREN'T PRUDES, but the three curates never discussed their sexual encounters with women. To some extent, it made them feel righteous within their limited understanding of the word. Alex was unable to articulate, Charles didn't want to boast and have it develop into a competition, and Brian was circumspect. They were more interested in what each other had to share on mundane issues.

This made it much more difficult for Alex to share his astonishing discovery with his two friends. He tried a couple of times and raised the subject of the dean's wife, but they didn't take the bait; his fishing encounters never hooked a response.

Eventually, he decided there was only one way to broach the subject. He'd tell them what he'd been doing with the dean's wife. At first neither responded, being reluctant to talk about their own involvement. There was also the issue of confidentiality. He began to think all he'd done was reveal his own indiscretion. But when he told them about the little blue book, they owned up. Of course, they had each been seduced, and it would never have gotten off the ground if they'd tried to come on to her. What a ridiculous notion!

Even though Alex was usually the least verbal, this situation had loosened his tongue. 'What the hell are we going to do? We can't just stop seeing her. She's kept records, so we're all in the shit.'

That got under Charles's skin, 'Well, you were in the perfect situation where you could have got the book. Why did you leave it there?'

'Don't blame it all on me. I didn't know what to do. It wasn't till after I got back here and told you guys that I realised it might have been a good idea.'

'You wouldn't have thought it was a good idea if we'd sent you a text message. Don't you ever think of anything else when using your dick?'

Brian intervened, suggesting there was no benefit in blaming each other. They were each implicated and needed to come up with a plan to save their careers.

They calmed down and discussed how they might sort it out, agreeing not to tell the dean upon his return from overseas. They also decided not to tell the bishop or the archbishop, as it would jeopardise their careers, which had hardly begun.

'That's great,' said Alex. 'All we've decided is who not to tell. Is there anyone else we shouldn't tell? How about the local TV station?'

'Well, I'm not telling my wife,' said Brian.

Alex was on the brink of walking out on his friends. He was never able to speak about things quickly enough to get a meaningful response. Even though Alex wanted to escape, he knew he was just as implicated as his two friends, so he stayed. His irritation approached breaking point.

'OK, let's go round and see her right now before we change our minds,' said Charles. 'Otherwise, we'll be talking about it forever.'

They agreed in silence as they stood and slowly walked to Charles's car.

'What will we say to her?' Alex wanted to know.

'Oh, for goodness' sake, Alex, stop trying to micromanage everything. It depends what she might say or do—she might not even be home—so any discussion about what we might say is a waste of time. Let's just play it by ear,' Charles said disdainfully.

'Well, I'm not saying anything,' said Alex.

'Tell us something we don't know,' said Charles.

They drove to the deanery in silence, deep in reflective thought.

All of a sudden, Alex spoke again. 'We have to get hold of the little blue book.'

'Brilliant deduction,' said Charles. 'Why don't you just run upstairs and get it while we chat to the dean's wife at the front door about the weather?'

Alex thought about that for a while, trying to work out if it was a serious suggestion.

None of them wanted to end the relationship with the dean's wife, and this development had only come about because they'd been exposed in the little blue book. As far as they knew, the blue book only implicated the three of them; but until they had a better look, it was a presumption. On the way, Alex got nervous again and said, 'What are we going to say then?'

'Give it a break.' Frustration was rising in all three.

'Let's see what she says when we get there.' Brian broke the silence. 'She'll be surprised to see all three of us on her doorstep together. As yet, she doesn't know we know we're all at it with her. So we have the element of surprise.'

It was dark when they pulled up opposite the deanery, but it appeared she'd already retired for the night because the only light on was in the bedroom. They all knew where the bedroom was. She already had a visitor because there was a car in the driveway, so they drove on past.

'That car', said Brian, 'belongs to the archbishop!'

As Charles was dropping them off, Alex had a thought. 'How come I was on page A but not the archbishop?'

'Because it's not his name, you bloody idiot, it's his title. Did you see the bishop on the next page, B, with Brian?'

'No,' said Alex, 'but he may not be having it off with the dean's wife.'

They each decided further discussion was a waste of time.

As their lives returned to some normality the issue of their indiscretions paled into insignificance following the dean's return home. As far as they were concerned, the passage of time would deal with the issue. They would deal with it by replacing past memories with new experiences, and they would get back into ministry. This was the reality of their world, which brought comfort. It became a subject unworthy of discussion as they agreed there was no solution. Their world had dealt with it, wrapped up in a single word—*denial* (not *sin*).

CHAPTER THIRTY-TWO

W HEN THE DEAN was home, the dean's wife needed to escape from domesticity. It wasn't that they got on each other's nerves; they just had nothing in common. She couldn't seek solace in her curates and took comfort in a spot in the local park.

Her favourite bench was by the duck pond. Weeping willow trees gently swayed in the afternoon breeze. There was a coffee lounge nearby, and she would usually get a takeaway and reflect on the issues important in her life.

I would never have thought three young men could be so different. I didn't expect them to be the same, but I can't help wondering why they are sexually poles apart. Brian is still embarrassed, cautious, and restrained. His initial reticence seems to have remained with him throughout our affair. I've not been able to develop his performance for my fulfilment.

He's always somewhere else emotionally when he's with me, and I thought I could change him from that characteristic. He always wants to leave when he's finished but stays as if it's too difficult to go, and yet I know he wants to go after he's achieved his climax. It seems to be a nervous disposition of insecurity, and yet he is the most confident of the three. In all other respects, he stands head and shoulders above the other two, and the dean has recognised this quality as a benefit to his plan of succession.

Charles, on the other hand, is not only ready to leave when he's had enough but just goes home. No discussion or excuse of having to be somewhere else. It almost makes me feel as if I'm being used. I find it surprisingly upsetting because I'm supposed to be using him. I even find it degrading to some extent. I thought he could be manipulated to do what I wanted him to do for me, but he's almost manipulating me!

Alex is just a sex machine, with an endless appetite. He's a sweet young man in his way and has the most voracious sexual appetite of all three. Insatiable and yet powerful. He never seems to tire, and I believe he could perform all night if I gave him the chance. I don't think I could keep up with him. I certainly want plenty of sex, but I like a day or two in between to recover. It's a peculiar experience in parting from all of them, almost as if they don't want to come again, except I know they do. Perhaps it's me!

CHAPTER THIRTY-THREE

A LEX APPROACHED HIS friends with a looming problem. His senior minister had given him the subject for him to preach his sermon—sexual immorality. 'Do you think he's found out what I've been doing?'

'Perhaps he's got hold of the dean's wife's little blue book,' Charles jested.

'How could that be unless he's been in the dean's wife's bedroom?'

'Oh, for goodness' sake, Charles, stop baiting him!' Brian chastised. 'Just do a Google search, and it will tell you what to say.'

'You know I don't know how to do that,' Alex complained, so Brian downloaded something and printed it out for him.

Brian's Google search told him to look at 1 Corinthians 6:18: 'Flee from sexual immorality. Every other sin a person commits is outside the body, but the sexually immoral person sins against his own body.'

'It's just between you and your own body. There's nothing to worry about. Problem solved,' was Brian's advice.

Of course, it wasn't what Alex was really worried about, it was confrontation with his congregation as they left the church, as he stood at the door to shake hands.

'Nobody's going to speak to you about it or challenge you. They'll simply accept it's a biblical theme the senior minister has given you to present as your sermon.' And so it was.

As Alex read from Brian's notes and looked around his 8.00 a.m. congregation, he was unable to see anyone under the age of seventy-five. This became easier than he thought. Not a single congregation member had the slightest inclination towards sex, let alone immoral sex.

His cage was rattled a little when a grey-haired couple stopped to exchange words at the door as they left church. Everyone else had passed through with just a handshake without comment, but his heart sank as the gentleman opened his mouth to speak.

'That was a difficult subject to preach,' the man said.

'Yes,' replied Alex, followed by a great sigh of relief.

Without realising, he was learning the ropes of non-definitive communication, which was to be developed over the ensuing years. Say less, listen more.

There were soon further developments in the ministry to confront the three young curates. They were told they were expected to lead groups within the congregation as part of their job. These involved a variety of subjects of biblical foundation, not the least of which was a group called Bible study.

The threesome met to discuss this development in their role as assistant ministers. Brian was not concerned, of course, and tried to explain to Alex how to deal with it. Charles was not particularly concerned. Brian was the first to lead a group, and his subject was the early church. His senior minister had given him notes from the Bible, based upon the narrative in the Acts of the Apostles. So what the senior minister had to say on the subject was already written for him. It was already written—in the Bible.

'What will you say when people ask questions?' was Alex's immediate reaction.

Brian was experienced in dealing with these situations. 'Why not come along as my guests, and you can see how I handle it.'

When Brian had presented his narrative from Acts, he invited the group of about fifteen people, mostly women, for discussion. A lady he recognised as the organist/piano player at services other than the main service launched into a question she considered very important. Her name was Gertrude, and she was the wife of one of the elders. Brian often saw her husband talking to the senior minister and thought he was one of the church council. Gertrude's husband collected and counted the offertory and always wore a suit and tie. *Probably the one he'd worn when he used to work for a living twenty years ago,* thought Brian.

'Yes, Gertrude, what is your question?'

'What is the point of knowing what the early church did 2,000 years ago? Life was different then without cars and roads and supermarkets. There weren't nearly as many people around then, so the needs of the population were nothing like they are today. What's the point of knowing all that stuff having absolutely nothing to do with how I manage to pay my electricity bill?'

She went on and on, asking question after question, and Brian never interrupted her. Alex became concerned about how he would deal with such a barrage when he led his own groups. Everyone had lost count of the number of questions Gertrude asked in her collage of verbiage. Brian was delighted to let her speak, because it limited the time others would have to ask questions. It also limited the time he'd have left to answer. When she'd eventually run out of steam, Brian looked around the table as they all looked to him for words of wisdom. His response was measured.

'Well, what do you think?' he asked the group.

Another lady who was clearly annoyed by the amount of time Gertrude had taken to ask her question, launched into her own list of questions having absolutely nothing to do with the early church.

'I want to know why God allows all these terrible things to happen in our world. If he's in control, why doesn't he control all these problems? My daughter in law . . .'

Brian loved this, he had no intention of even attempting to answer any questions, and the various clashes of personalities in his congregation had developed into a pressure release valve for them. It inevitably consumed the two hours allocated for the group meeting.

This was to become a standard response for Brian. Instead of answering the question, he responded with a question. His intent to encourage them to share opinion as well as diverting their questions away from him was his developing strategy. Christians were too polite to query why the leader hadn't answered. They considered that their positions as congregational members was to be led, not to lead.

After about two hours, the discussion lost momentum, and Brian thanked everyone.

'This has been a very worthwhile discussion, and I hope you've all found something useful from the group. We'll meet again next week, same place, same time. Now how about joining us for a cup of tea or coffee and a biscuit before you go home?'

'You didn't answer a single question, what was the point?' Alex commented after the group had all gone. Brian's response was to be a major lesson for Alex as well as Charles.

'You don't have to answer any questions. You simply act as sort of a chairman and encourage them to share. It's what they want to do, so it's not difficult. It's sort of a clearing house for issues they want to get off their chest, especially with their minister present.'

There were further developments of this learning curve for them all, but at this stage, it was sufficient.

They hadn't received any invitations from the dean's wife for about six months because the dean was home. However, they'd been so busy with all the extra activities within the church calendar that they were quietly looking forward to his next trip.

CHAPTER THIRTY-FOUR

WHEN THE DEAN was home, he accelerated his succession training with Brian and encouraged him to take up positions on boards of trustees, who, the dean said, were looking for younger men to become involved. This was, of course, the dean's agenda; it had nothing to do with what trustees had suggested.

'Current trustees are past their use-by date,' said the dean during training. 'We need to get rid of some of the old-timers. They're negatively influencing agenda towards progress.'

Committee or trustees had no idea the dean planned to fill a vacancy he would create by getting rid of someone of his choice.

'You need to understand, Brian—these trusts aren't in the name of the church, but being a trustee enables us to exercise discretionary power to direct funds to support the church's financial needs.'

A legal representative who sat on the committee purely in an advisory capacity and with no voting power was aware of discretionary trusts being only as good as the people who served as trustees.

'I want to tell how things get done around here,' said the dean in the privacy of his office. 'You've been in on a few meetings and heard the type of discussions where certain elders want to direct money from the account to causes mentioned in the deed of trust. That's all very well, but I've got plans to get things going in this diocese. We are spending far too much time talking about things other than where I want to direct the money. I plan to introduce more young people on to the committee so we can get these things through more efficiently. It will mean some older members will have to go, but without encouragement, they'll stay forever and probably outlive me.'

'How can I help?' said Brian, wanting to appear compliant.

'I just want you to support motions I make to move things forward. Even if you have an opinion, just observe and take my lead.'

'How will you get the old guys to resign?' asked Brian.

'It's not as difficult as it might appear. First of all, I'll enter an item during any other business, with a suggestion. We're all getting older, myself included, and we should start to plan succession. We should bring on to the committee young and inexperienced members and bring them up to speed. They won't disagree with such a proposal. *Succession* is a modern word for, "Get out of the way you, old buggers, and let some new ideas into the system."'

The dean shared more of his strategy. 'Step one is to get them to agree to a succession plan. Step two, I'll bring along a guest—a young man, of course—who'll come to see what it's all about. In the meantime, I'll talk to a couple of the other trustees and massage one old guy out at a time. We have to start slowly, but within a year, we should have a new and young board of trustees.'

The dean's hidden agenda was, the young men he'd chosen wouldn't dare vote against anything the dean suggested. The dean would then have control.

The dean welcomed the board of trustees and opened the meeting, 'Thank you, gentlemen, for attending, I'm sorry to have kept you all waiting. Another meeting dragged on and on! Let's open with prayer. Heavenly Father, we commit this meeting to you and ask your guidance in our thoughts and words as we share in appropriating the distribution of funds to your praise and glory. Amen.'

What a load of cobblers, thought Brian. *You've planned what you're going to say before you even said the prayer. You don't believe this stuff any more than I do.*

The dean continued. 'We have a guest today, but he's only here as an observer and to see what we do in service to the church, so our meeting will be conducted as normal. His name is Anthony Briar, and perhaps you may have heard him on his Christian radio chat talk-back show on station 7WGH. First item on the agenda is the public address system in the cathedral. Now we all know this is pretty bad and is long overdue for replacement.'

'No, it isn't,' said one of the old-timers. 'We spent $80,000 on it only two years ago.'

The dean bridled. 'That doesn't alter the fact that it doesn't work very well, so we need to get it replaced.'

'So what's the item on the agenda, fix it or replace it?' the old guy added.

This guy has to be at the top of the list to move him on, Brian thought.

'The issue surely is the PA is useless, and one way or another, it has to be rectified. I take it nobody disagrees with that,' said the dean as he brought the meeting back to order.

'We agreed to spend $80,000 two years ago, so who ordered the equipment which you're now saying is no good?' Except the man knew who had ordered the system—the discussion was developing into war of words challenging the dean in front of committee.

'OK,' said the dean, 'I propose we set up a working committee and employ a specialist public address company to come and do a report and recommend a resolution. This puts the action outside my area of influence.'

They mumbled around the table again as trustees chatted amongst themselves, so the dean said, 'Well, that's settled then.'

'No, it isn't,' said the objector. 'How much is that going to cost? We're supposed to be administering this money through consensus and wisdom as custodians of God's provision. Unless we are seen to be transparent and do things correctly, history will repeat itself.'

'OK,' said the dean. 'Let's set a budget for an expert to come and give us advice. So how much shall we say, $10,000 or $20,000?'

The old guy exploded. 'That's ridiculous. I'm not suggesting a budget for someone to come and give advice. I'm suggesting a budget to fix the problem. You get three companies experienced in public address systems to come and give us a quote. First to fix the system we already have, and second to replace the old system if they consider repairs unviable. We don't pay them for giving us a quote. They make their money if we accept their quote. This will keep them competitive.'

'It's getting late, and we aren't making progress, let's set up a working committee and get them to report back to us at the next meeting,' suggested the dean.

'OK, provided it doesn't cost us any money, and I would like it recorded in the minutes.'

Even though the objector mumbled on, he was outvoted on the issue of the working committee. The dean's influence took control as usual.

'Brian, will you please chair a working committee and involve Mr Jackson and Mr Gordon? We don't need more than three, or we'll never get this thing resolved.'

Nobody seemed to notice the dean had selected the working committee and put Brian in control of it!

When they'd all gone, the dean debriefed Brian.

'You see what I mean?' said the dean. 'We've twelve trustees, and only one guy was difficult. If we vote him off the board, we can get meetings over more effectively. There's another young man I know who writes for a Christian newspaper. I'll have a word with him and see if he's prepared to serve on committee. He doesn't know anything, but he'll be attracted to the idea of sitting as a trustee to serve the church. It'll make him feel important, and he'll do what we want him to do. We can explain our needs outside any meeting so he comes forearmed and votes as we want him to.'

Brian considered the old gentleman was correct, but he wasn't about to voice his opinion to the trustees and especially not in front of the dean. The dean seemed to be in his job for very similar reasons to Brian, so he could hardly criticise.

Both the dean and Brian considered they were discreet. But in fact, most of the trustees were aware and weren't prepared to challenge his authority. However, it was a much deeper issue because Brian's ignorance of anything spiritual enabled him to support the dean. Brian's future depended on it!

The diocese had been influenced by the dean's faith, which was entirely cerebral, supported by ever-conservative church chapter members. It was a brave man who'd challenge the dean's agenda. One was either for him or against him. Any expectations of advancement were clearly never going to happen unless one was compliant! The benefit for Brian would be the luxuries of high office. He almost felt appreciative that their motivation was similar—self-centred.

Typically, church congregations might have believed appointments in the church were consistent with a transparent selection process, and this was certainly the intended disclosure by the hierarchy. So things only appeared to be transparent, although truthfully more like it was covered with a veil clouding biblical truth, instead of allowing to see through the glass clearly.

So the succession plan continued its inevitable path, which, fortunately for Brian, crossed paths with the dean's wife on no few occasions. One of the interesting things about their relationship was the complete absence of dialogue. It was all body language, even to the point of sexual fulfilment. It wasn't like the first time, when she'd asked him if he'd enjoyed sex and he'd made a response about the pope. He wasn't thinking!

CHAPTER THIRTY-FIVE

T HE DEAN'S WIFE never sent text invitations to the curates. She was aware text messages were held in the cell phone memory as well in the archives of the Internet service provider (ISP).

She was also sufficiently IT savvy enough to know, deleted messages only removed text from an active file into the trash bin. Unless the trash bin was emptied, messages were there forever. She'd also learnt that even if text messages were deleted from the trash bin, they still existed in the ISP archives. If records of her indiscretions were to be deleted, she would have to empty her active file and her trash bin as well as the ISP archives by both the sender and the receiver. If just one message was not deleted correctly, it could provide evidence of a trail she didn't want anyone to know about.

As a consequence, invitations from her cell phone were always verbal, identified as a blocked number. She recognised their voices and would simply say a time, usually in the afternoon. The venue had changed from her home to a motel about three suburbs away from the deanery—sufficiently distant so her car wasn't recognised but not too far to waste time driving.

Motels were all very similar, and she had checked several places on the premise of vetting for some friends who planned to visit. Cost was not too relevant, and she was not interested in facilities like a TV, DVD players, or even a telephone. Since the advent of cell phones, landlines in motels were disappearing. Cleanliness was her priority, shown, for example by having decent towels in the bathroom. She also liked the location to be off the main road with parking round the back, out of sight of any passing traffic. The motel selected had a large bedroom with a king-sized bed and bedside tables with lamps screwed down so they couldn't be stolen. A large flowery print above the bed was also screwed to the wall. One redeeming feature of her chosen motel was the fitted carpet. Mostly they were encrusted with dropped food and drink from takeaways. A vacuum cleaner never cleaned up that sort of mess. This motel must have replaced the carpet recently because it was clean and soft. There was nothing worse than stepping out of the shower and walking barefoot on crusty, dirty carpet.

Brian had been invited one afternoon, and he was first on her list! She always arrived half an hour before the appointed time to settle in and have a hot shower. She would then put on a negligee to tantalise her trainees. Brian's expectations were always high, and he was aroused before he even arrived at the motel. She needed more arousal than just anticipation. She would tease him when he arrived.

'Brian, how lovely to see you again. Would you like a drink from the minibar? He was much too polite to say he'd not come for a drink and just wanted to get on with it.

'Let me take your jacket.' She would slowly undress him, leaving his underpants, which didn't hide his embarrassment due to an erection. His embarrassment disappeared when they came off, but his erection didn't. So she let him linger in his state of embarrassment. It was all part of her enjoyment.

'Do you like my negligee?' It was a rhetorical question because Brian was always uncommunicative. His body language said everything that needed saying. Even when she pulled the top cover off the bed, she was measured in her closeness, a touch here, a touch there. She was familiar with Brian's sexual responses as she triggered each sense of feel and touch. Not a touch that started and continued towards the inevitable, but a touch that started and stopped. She was such a tease.

Brian just stood in anticipation, reluctant to make any moves towards the bed. He appeared to be the least experienced and needed more direction than the other two. Charles was clearly more experienced but still had much to learn. Alex was instinctively lustful, and her bull in the china shop. She had great difficulty holding him back.

Brian's mind flashed back to his first encounter with the dean's wife. It was a mixture of guilt and enthusiastic anticipation. His sexual activity with Sally was never anticipated. He would come home from church in hope, even expectation, but she'd be asleep. Domesticity ruled Sally's life, and her responses were dull. The excitement he'd discovered with the dean's wife overruled any guilt. These thoughts were never articulated, either with Sally or the dean's wife. He hardly understood it himself.

My married life with Sally is like living in a cage, restricted by an immovable barrier, and yet sometimes I can escape my cage into the arms of the dean's wife.

CHAPTER THIRTY-SIX

B RIAN WAS NURTURING his reacquaintance with Carlos, the assistant minister with the Catholic church. He'd responded to a personal invitation to catch up with his schoolboy chum. It was hardly a friendship but a relationship which might be useful one day.

He was the same age as Brian, except Carlos had incredible dress sense. His ecclesiastical attire reflected a physical fitness showing off his other attractive features. *Surely a magnet for the girls,* thought Brian.

'So what's your poison, Brian? Scotch, gin, wine, or beer?'

Even though he'd been here before, it didn't seem right somehow to drink alcohol in a church building. *But what the heck, and why not anyway?*

'Scotch and ice please, Carlos, and plenty of ice.'

They sat down in plush armchairs, and Brian couldn't help thinking what he could offer Carlos if he visited him in his church office. They would be sitting on plastic chairs, and the only drink he could offer would be instant coffee served in a cardboard takeaway cup. Of course, this saved washing the cup afterwards, but it impacted Brian in the contradictions of his church life.

'So what do you do in your spare time?' enquired Carlos.

'Spare time, what spare time?'

'Don't you go to a show, live music, see a movie?' Carlos seemed to have a life outside the church.

The only thing he could think was to say, 'I'm married and have two kids, so I have a lot of personal commitments at home.' Brian felt nervous about the celibacy issue because everything about his life involved the very things Carlos was denied.

'I can't remember when I last saw a movie or went to a show,' Brian almost whispered, hardly wanting to accept his seemingly boring domestic life. He was actually thinking more about his relationship with the dean's wife. So much so that his concentration for meaningful discussion dried up. They found common ground in cricket and spoke about international test matches and the short-over games.

'Would you like another scotch?' asked Carlos.

'Don't mind if I do, thanks,' said Brian. 'Do all Catholic churches have cocktail cabinets in the church office to entertain guests?' *In such comfortable lounges with recliners in such style,* he thought, but didn't say.

'Oh yes, this is normal,' said Carlos. 'We're living in the real world and enjoy the same things like everyone else. Well, almost.'

Brian again wondered how he coped with celibacy, but it was a bit soon in their relationship to go into something so personal.

This new experience for Brian was not limited to the comfort of the surroundings. He'd been so impressed with Carlos's style of clothes. The crease in his trousers—perfect, as was the length, style, and cut. *No way his came off the peg,* he thought. It reminded him of James Heddington's well-cut bespoke suit.

Brian couldn't help noticing Carlos had something else in his persona apart from having his collar back to front and his smartness, but he'd no idea what it was. Charisma came to mind. He thought the friendship might become useful, apart from having a free cocktail bar handy instead of the Pig and Whistle. If nothing else, his new relationship challenged his dress sense. He'd been encouraged by the dean to present himself in casual attire, which meant a clean open-necked shirt, jeans, and black shoes. This casual presentation wasn't limited to social church functions but also in church services, and so the pulpit was no longer the place to present a sermon robed up. Sermons were now performed without gowns and from the lectern, down at the same level as the congregation.

His senior minister justified the change in church protocol as moving away from the old-fashioned church, where ministers were somehow elevated above the congregation. The same thing applied to dressing up with collars back to front. Brian was able to understand the psychology, except by not having them, it didn't seem to increase the numbers in his congregation. He also wondered if there was supposed to be some sort of spiritual element in Christianity, but this thought didn't linger long in his reflective mind. His senior minister's psychology made more sense to him than theological theory.

Carlos invited Brian into his church. It was the first time he'd been inside a Catholic church. In the same way he'd noticed Carlos's personal style of dress, he instantly noticed a difference inside the Catholic church. It had an immediate impact upon him.

'What are all these stained glass windows everywhere?' enquired Brian.

Carlos explained they were known as the Stations of the Cross. Each picture depicted Jesus life leading up to the Crucifixion. Carlos didn't think there was need to explain and was rather surprised even to have been asked. After all, Brian was an ordained minister, notwithstanding he was an assistant minister. As they walked down the centre aisle, Brian noticed the big table resplendent in its size and beauty. The top seemed to be a single piece of hardwood polished to a mirror finish. But it was the ornate carved legs which made the table so impressive.

'The altar table,' said Carlos, as he remembered the Anglican cathedral had removed its altar table and, in fact, all icons from inside the cathedral. They walked around in silence, neither of them thinking there was any more to say. Brian reflected upon the complete absence of icons in his own church as well as his cathedral—there was not even a cross. Apart from the Stations of the Cross, the Catholic church displayed a cross with Jesus hanging upon it. The Anglican church used to display an empty cross, which Brian understood was symbolic of the risen Christ, but now even the cross was gone. Brian's interpretation was one of simplific justification. One less thing to try and explain to his congregation, a bit like so many church symbols studied in church history during his seminary days, now forgotten.

Carlos was well informed, and when they returned to the ambience of his office lounge, he asked Brian, 'Why did your dean remove everything iconic from the Anglican cathedral? Was it intended to direct parish churches to follow his lead?'

'I don't know,' said Brian. 'It all happened before my time.'

Brian was out of his depth even though he'd studied church history, which for him was one of the issues irrelevant about church. However, it had given him insight into the power the dean had in getting rid of tradition. His relationship with his Catholic friend enabled him to have some perspective of the differences between the Catholic and Anglican churches, something he'd never even thought about before, and why would he?

Brian's understanding of diminishing numbers in church congregations reflected a cerebral understanding, which had nothing to do with clerical clothing or church adornments, iconic or otherwise. The decline was taking place irrespective, in both Anglican and Catholic churches.

In no small measure, Brian was embarrassed in his relationship with Carlos, who was attentive and looked him straight in the eye. For reasons not understood by Brian, he'd developed relationships without eye contact. This had first come to his attention when meeting the dean's wife, during which he was eye-locked and heading towards seduction. Carlos was another person making eye contact with him in a very personal way. Brian didn't realise he'd developed a style of communication where he avoided eye contact. When he was speaking publicly to a crowd, it wasn't necessary to make eye contact because it wasn't personal. It was collective. This was how he'd addressed his congregation, with distant engagement, and this was how he addressed personal contacts.

He was unaware of it because it was the way he'd been tutored, not to get involved with anyone in his congregation. The dean was like it too, so it wasn't surprising Brian had developed a similar style. Such behaviour was so normal, so natural it followed him at functions such as fetes and fund-raising events.

He would present in his casual attire, clean-shaven and with modest haircut. He had no tattoos (at least none visible) or what generation Y referred to as body piercing. He'd learnt the courteous manner of recognising someone and appearing to be pleased to see them. He could have a discussion without actually listening to what they were saying.

They spoke to him, but his eyes wandered around the room and his ears were closed. He never engaged in any meaningful conversation. Then after a short period, he'd say, most politely, 'Would you please excuse me, I need to speak to so and so over there.' And off he'd go. People found this extremely rude, and because he wasn't actually listening, he would excuse himself halfway through a sentence, not realising what he was doing. More to the point, he didn't care.

CHAPTER THIRTY-SEVEN

ANOTHER INVITATION TO attend the deanery for dinner included the three curates, during which the dean announced his impending trip overseas on another lecture tour. This time it would be possible to follow him on his blog page, which would also show anyone who cared to follow his trail. They could also listen to his presentations on MP3. It never occurred to him that nobody cared.

'We'll be able to keep track of his return date,' Charles whispered to Brian. It would herald the end of their next series of sexual transgressions with the dean's wife.

'Surely, the church should be getting involved in all this high-tech stuff.' Brian's mind was developing cyberspace thoughts he shared with Charles. It was beyond Alex's mental ability, and they purposely excluded him.

Charles had a light-switch moment. 'The traditional church will lose these growing cyber-savvy congregations to charismatic denominations who promote their own Christian singers on recording labels they also own. Merchandising on the Internet is big business.'

Brian agreed. 'The Internet offers an opportunity to contact a much wider audience than just an attendant congregation. The dean is already doing it at least in part, having his own blog and social media sites.'

Brian withdrew from active ministry and devoted time developing his own website, but this was only the start. It consumed much of his time, about which he already suffered overload. He thought the dean would be impressed if he launched his own parish website—the first and most important part of which (in his opinion) was to design a logo.

'We have to have a logo,' Brian told his church council. 'This will be something everyone will associate with our church. It will put us on the cyber map! It's symbolic. It's like a badge of honour or a coat of arms. I'll design it, so it won't cost the church anything.' Who could disagree with that?

Brian was very proud of his logo and would show anybody expressing the slightest interest in what he was doing in his new cyber ministry. Although he didn't actually say as much, his logo was more important than anything else, because it was his design. The website was launched, and he posted his sermons on it week by week. Instead of naming his blog page St Aiden's, it would be more appropriate to call it Braithwaite Ministries. He was blissfully unaware, however, that nobody ever logged into his blog to read his renditions, so it didn't adversely affect his ego.

CHAPTER THIRTY-EIGHT

B RIAN BECAME CRITICAL of the drinks selection at the dean's dinner functions. The choice of wine was red or white. If he'd been with his Catholic friend Carlos for dinner, the choice would've been, Shiraz or Cabernet Sauvignon, Riesling, Pinot Grigio, Chardonnay, or Sauvignon Blanc.

'Red or white,' he mumbled under his breath. 'Where's their wine etiquette?'

Brian's relationship with Carlos developed as he accepted a few social outings with him. He was surprised how Carlos changed when he wasn't wearing his clerical garb. He was still very smartly dressed, but no one would guess he was a clergyman. Brian was unable to make this transition, and his career had made him a clergyman both in church and private social life. This was quite amazing, really, because Brian was as secular as they come.

Carlos had invited Brian to a jazz concert, just the two of them, at the end of which they went back to Carlos's cocktail bar for a nightcap. This time, Brian noted it was even more palatial than his own home.

Brian felt comfortable now to raise the issue of celibacy. 'I saw you with a girl during the interval, Carlos. How do you deal with those situations?'

Carlos didn't understand and answered simply, 'I didn't have any difficulty. She was a very attractive girl, and she spoke informatively about the bands we'd just seen.'

'I didn't mean that,' said Brian. 'How do you handle the next stage?'

'What next stage? I was talking to her about the music.'

'Well, what if she wanted to take the relationship further and you were pressed for a date? How do you deal with celibacy?'

'Oh that,' said Carlos. 'As Christians, we both understand what it means to take a vow before God. As a priest I've taken vows, like you've taken vows when you got married. Your vows committed you to have a sexual relationship with your wife and she with you, to the exclusion of all others. You honour those vows, don't you? I honour my vows in exactly the same way as I have vowed celibacy before God. So if a girl "comes on strong" as you might put it, I would tell her I'm a Catholic priest and have vowed to honour my body in celibacy. I guess you'd do the same if a girl came on to you. You'd tell her you were already married and your vows prevented you from having any intimate relationship other than with your wife.'

Carlos was, of course, unaware of Brian's extramarital relationship, but it was a moral blow to his dignity and put him in his place. Carlos had simply answered the question, having no idea behind Brian's inquisition. At least Brian now understood how Carlos handled his celibacy—no doubt about it!

He'd been quite looking forward to the dean's latest trip before Carlos had enlightened him about celibacy. However, he soon got over it since clearly it offered a sexual release from the restraints he experienced in marriage. Sally had become even less imaginative in bed recently, even though he hadn't lost his appetite. It was clear the dean's wife was going in the opposite direction to Sally in terms of libido, substance, and longevity.

Brian's earlier sexual encounters with the dean's wife had been fulfilling, but now he was beginning to feel physically tired after the event. He wondered if he was getting past it. She seemed to grow in her demands for extended periods of sexual activity, and sometimes he would like to have said enough was enough. But he couldn't. His pride wouldn't let him.

The three curates were now comparing notes, not so much on performance but on the actual dates of their respective encounters. They were becoming more frequent, and instead of a week between each of them, they'd closed up to a couple of days. No one was complaining— after all, they each had their needs, and she called the shots. They didn't turn up when their libido beckoned; they turned up when the dean's wife beckoned.

CHAPTER THIRTY-NINE

WHEREAS THE HIERARCHY of the church believed Alex's ministry was successfully active, he'd been getting into trouble. He'd always liked a bit of a flutter on the horses—or in fact, anything to bring in a monetary windfall. It had nothing to do with his financial needs; it was an emotional reaction. He'd had the occasional win, nothing substantial, but a win among so many losses kept the enthusiasm fuelled. Brian and Charles weren't aware of this, but it was no big deal.

Alex's taste for gambling had developed as a consequence of mastering the cell phone. He could bet without having to visit a TAB. He'd downloaded a free app, and losses were debited directly out of his bank account.

He hadn't consulted Brian about his enjoyment to gamble and drink, and why should he when it wasn't a problem? Well, it wasn't a problem to start with, but it had developed into a problem. Alex had become involved beyond his ability to pay his debts, which were mounting. He'd dealt with this by getting another credit card, which was easy enough because banks were falling over themselves to issue them.

His first refinancing solution was to get another credit card to pay the interest on the card in debt. Amazingly, he was able to get five cards during his escape from reality and do the same thing over again, but he'd built up debts totalling $20,000 and had no more credit cards available. He was too embarrassed to approach Brian and tried his bank manager for help. He didn't have to say why he wanted a loan since as a clergyman with no mortgage or other serious overheads, as well as a secure salary, the bank welcomed him with open arms as a low-risk client.

The bank manager said, 'How about $20,000? Unsecured, of course, as a personal loan?' So the interest rate was a bit high, but

Alex wasn't concerned about the rate. That could worry about itself tomorrow.

It was one of those situations to save the day, except as usual Alex was unable to foresee the consequences of default in his interest payments, let alone the capital debt. With $20,000 at his disposal, he decided to win back his losses and discharge his credit card debts. He had a plan. However, he didn't know how it happened. One day he had $20,000, and a couple of days later, it was all gone! Now he was $40,000 in debt.

As usual, he was unable to talk to his parents. He couldn't speak to his bishop or archbishop. Men of the cloth just don't do things as stupid as borrowing money and gambling with it. Of course, it wouldn't have been a problem if he'd won, but he was unable to see the consequences of his actions until the increased debt was a reality. ADHD had raised its ugly head again. In desperation, he turned to Brian, who, of course, was able to deal with the problem.

Brian visited each creditor in turn, attired in his new classic-style ecclesiastical shirt and collar and impeccably tailored trousers, a reflection of his friend Carlos. As a minister of the church, he commanded respect. It used to be a bank manager who was the pinnacle of perceived respectability in the community, but in this case, the boot was on the other foot.

Brian's approach to each bank was authoritative. 'You have provided a fellow clergyman with a line of credit without establishing his ability to repay and were only concerned with the interest the debt generated, which could go on almost for eternity. The bank has two options. The first is for my colleague to declare bankruptcy, in which case you won't get a cent of interest or any of the capital. The bank will have to write this off as a bad debt against your branch.'

He paused for what seemed like a minute, but it was only a few seconds. The impact was the same with each bank manager. Before continuing, he wanted each manager to reflect upon his responsibility and more particularly his accountability.

'The second option', he continued, 'is to freeze the account. This will prevent it moving in your ledger from a loan to a bad debt. My colleague will pay a notional amount every month to discharge the capital. This will take a long time, perhaps as long as the term of interest you had imposed.' Brian presented it in such a way as to infer it was non-negotiable.

Alex could no longer use his credit cards, of course, but that was the least of his problems. All creditors agreed to the ultimatum. Brian had solved Alex's dilemma once again. By now Brian was much more familiar with ADHD. Charles still had no idea. Goodness knows what might've happened if the bishop or archbishop had found out. They would have surely defrocked him for gambling with borrowed money. The glue that bonded them together became even stronger!

CHAPTER FORTY

THEIR CURACIES HAD developed in a blur of memories, and within two years, they each had their own parish as senior ministers. It was normal for senior minister vacancies to be advertised in the Christian press. Applicants came from a variety of clerics looking for a change of parish. It wasn't only assistant ministers looking for positions vacant but also senior ministers looking for a change of parish. It also drew applicants from outside the diocese. The selection process was presented to follow a transparent procedure, but in reality, influence was brought to bear behind the scenes, even before any vacancies were advertised.

The dean contributed to this process behind closed doors. His unwritten directive successful applicants should've been trained in his diocesan college carried weight. Ministers coming from colleges outside his diocese had been known to bring some disturbing biblical interpretations. He was just trying to deal with any prospective issues before they happened. Usually it was decided who would be appointed to whichever parish before interview. Church council would be involved in a process but were sufficiently distant from the machinations of hierarchy to be aware of these prior negotiations.

Parish church council would interview prospective applicants and make their recommendation to the dean, who would exercise his opinion through acceptance or rejection. He was not accountable, so he never gave any reasons why a particular applicant might be unacceptable. Consequently, the dean controlled appointees whom he considered best for the particular challenges needing attention in a parish. There were prestigious parishes to which almost every applicant wanted to be appointed, as there were others to which nobody wanted to be appointed. The latter might be an inner-city problem spot where drugs and alcohol created many church and social problems. The archbishop rarely got involved other than under extenuating circumstances, one of which did cross his desk.

Brian had exercised his influence with the archbishop to ensure his own appointment to a prestigious parish. St Aiden's was his choice, having titles over a number of retail shops adjacent to the church, drawing significant and regular rentals.

St Aiden's could survive financially without any offertories. The issue with just about every other parish was that it fell upon the senior minister and his staff (if he had any) to raise funds for regular submission to the diocese. The intent being, these funds would be consolidated and redistributed to less financially viable parishes to effect a degree of equalisation.

The cost of church building maintenance and running costs continually rose due to inflation combined with the age of heritage church buildings. Offertories usually diminished due to reduced attendances and was also influenced by aged congregations having limited expendable income as pensions failed to keep up with inflation.

Brian quickly fitted into his new parish mainly because of his organisational skills, which he'd refined during his assistant ministry posting. Grooming by the dean also contributed. He'd also fine-tuned his appearance from what he'd noticed from his Catholic friend. He'd discovered where Carlos bought his tailored clothes and splashed out on a complete new outfit. St Aidan's was a parish without any financial problems.

Because Brian was tidy, cleanly dressed, and personable, the congregation accepted him—not that they really had any choice in the selection process, with Brian having been recommended by the archbishop and rubber-stamped by the dean.

Life had moved on for Brian in a stable and comfortable way. There were no challenges from the church council other than his choice of churchwarden. The incumbent was in advancing years, with a good knowledge and experience of the parish, but he was two generations distant from Brian, who wanted to appoint someone his own age. In any event, it was Brian's prerogative, so any objection from the church council was simply out of order. Brian wanted to change the image of his parish to attract generation Y because they weren't only more compatible with his lifestyle, they had more expendable income to contribute to the offertory.

The dean expected congregational growth under Brian's leadership, supported by an increase in funds to contribute to the diocese. Plans to increase the congregation were colloquially referred to as 'bums on seats'. The congregation Brian inherited was predominantly old-age pensioners and, clearly, a dying proportion of any prospective offertory source.

He asked Sally, 'How do you think I could increase my congregation?' He had his own ideas, but he liked to include her in church issues whenever he could.

'Why don't you share the responsibility with the declining congregation? Make them feel it's their responsibility. Tell them you have plans to grow the kingdom, without telling them how. That will appeal to their sense of duty. Then tell them you want them each to bring two people to church next Sunday—neighbours, friends, or family. If they all did it, the congregation would immediately swell from 60 to 180. Problem solved. Anyway, some of them might respond, and it might work, at least in part.'

He'd planned to remove the old wooden pews and replace them with more comfortable chairs. *Carlos would surely approve,* he thought. The intent was to make the old church building user-friendly. This would not only enable more chairs to be accommodated as the congregation grew but also offer flexible layouts to suit different church activities.

The church council reacted in opposition and called a meeting to dissuade the new minister from taking out their lovely timber pews. The bishop sent his troubleshooter to put out the 'bush fire'. Brian chaired the meeting, of course, under the dean's directive.

'Thank you all for coming. Perhaps we could start by our bishop's special envoy explaining his purpose in coming.'

The meeting was respectfully quiet through the preamble. Brian then invited members to ask questions, and the meeting erupted.

One old-timer was the loudest and most persistent. 'Sixty years ago just after the war, the congregation was asked to contribute financially to have pews handmade out of western red cedar. It's a beautiful timber difficult and costly to get now, even if you could buy red cedar. And now you want to chuck them away and get something modern. Those who contributed back then gave out of their poverty, not out of their riches. It's disgraceful even to suggest removal.'

Others were so passionate about having their say. Everyone wanted to contribute, and a lady shared her point between floods of tears. 'I'm sorry to be so emotional. But this is completely unnecessary, and I'm very upset about it. Why can't we just leave things as they are?'

The anger built up as each had their say, both Brian and the bishop sat quietly listening, making no response. Brian's thoughts drifted away to the dean's directive. 'Always appoint yourself chairman,' he'd said. 'Then you have control. Let people talk about their differences, and then wind up the meeting so everyone thinks they have contributed. Never lose sight of your own objective.'

The bishop's representative had the last say. 'It's very important you share your concerns. However, the diocese has to focus on the big picture. It's not just the parish or even the diocese, it's the kingdom. Everything we do at the head office has a financial implication. It's unfortunate, but it's the reality of the world in which we live. To ignore it would disable the entire structure of the church. I understand your concerns, but in his way, your minister is working towards diocesan objectives, which is to encourage new attendees to church, new souls to be saved. Then we can preach the gospel to more people. The church has to change, and I understand people don't like change. I hope you will find it in your hearts to support your minister as he deals with these changes.'

Bums on seats, thought Brian. If he'd remembered his church history, biblical narrative recorded Jesus didn't try and get people into church buildings. Jesus went *out* preaching the good news of the kingdom.

Brian's mind drifted away from the meeting, recollecting a true story. A minister wanted to move the piano from one side of the church to the other. Without consulting anyone, he moved it a foot each month, eventually arriving on the other side of the church. It went without notice.

It was quite amazing how Brian was able to arrange the removal of the pews even though nothing had been agreed at the meeting. After their removal, he put half the chairs out with a little space between them. The church looked full. As bums increased, he would close up spaces and place more chairs. The ornate terracotta tiles were overlaid with fitted carpet throughout the church. This would improve the acoustics for when the band was installed. In the end, it looked like a church from the outside but like a social club on the inside.

Rather than choose chairs from a local supplier, Brian employed a colour and decorator consultant. He'd no idea of colour or décor, and if an expert was employed, it would insulate him from any criticism or accountability if perchance there were any objections. He'd learnt this strategy at Heddingtons. Accountability was always an issue when spending someone else's money—in this case, the church parish's money.

The chairs were expensive, and airfreight from overseas significantly affected the unit cost. They weren't only expensive by local standards; the unit cost approximated four times what could have been purchased locally. Brian wrapped up the cost of chairs with consultancy, décor, and all the other costs. The parish had plenty of cash, so it wasn't an issue. Plans cost money too, and all this effort would be worthwhile when the extra congregational members contributed towards the offertory. If the congregation were pleased with the result, he would take credit. If not, he could join them and shoot arrows of discontent at the consultant. He'd been well taught how to protect his back.

He also had plans to introduce more modern songs to replace the old-fashioned hymns. Part of his plan involved establishing a band to liven up the services, which in turn would attract the younger generation. There might be some objections from the ageing congregation, but since they were ever diminishing, he could easily justify his plans. His first step was to appoint his own warden, which of course signalled the retirement of the incumbent. Next, he would introduce young applicants for church council, who would make changes he planned for church services. He wanted to discontinue the 8.00 a.m. service of Holy Communion, but initially, he would continue to conduct it exactly the same as his predecessor. This would be a service of Holy

Communion, old-fashioned hymns, an organist, even the 1662 Book of Common Prayer. As the numbers continued to diminish through natural attrition, he would eventually close the service down. By which time, the younger-generation services (with a band) at 10.00 a.m. would be the main family service.

He'd learnt that changing anything had to be done in small steps instead of doing it all at once. Change was a difficult issue in the church; he was able to manipulate changes a little at a time, forever moving towards his ultimate objective.

He never shared his plans with anyone, not even his new warden or church council. This would have resulted in useless discussion. What they didn't know, they wouldn't worry about. He had been taught well.

Without realising, Brian's change of church structure was strengthening his resolve to control other areas in his life. He was becoming more like the dean every day. His relationship with the dean's wife was also changing.

CHAPTER FORTY-ONE

ALEX HAD A very different ministry from his two friends. It would be difficult for anyone to think these three ministers were in the same institution. During his curacy, he'd been exposed to people who existed on the fringes of society. Alex gravitated towards them since he saw himself as being one only step away from their affliction.

He needed support and decided to have a chat with Brian. 'I'm feeling vulnerable with these people in my congregation. I know you warned me about this, but it's just happened. They've become dependent on me for just about everything because they have nothing.'

'That's a very profound observation, Alex, and it should make you feel proud. You've achieved a great deal for these people, especially since nobody else cares.'

'Yes, I know, but I feel more and more like one of them. Most of my day is dealing with their needs, one way or another.'

Alex was close to breakdown by thinking if he became one of them, who would look after him?

'Why don't I come and visit you and your congregation one evening for dinner. Let me see what's going on?'

Brian was good to his word and walked in on the evening meal. The smell of unwashed bodies and urine-soaked clothing was overpowering. Many had come in from the rain with wet clothes, and this added to the odour combined with the smell of vegetable soup. Brian couldn't help watching a woman slowly eating her soup and bread roll. She looked about seventy, but looks could be deceiving. *Is she someone's mother, someone's sister? Had she been married and once had a home, a family, somewhere warm to sleep?* Brian's thoughts drifted around the room as he realised the same questions could apply to everyone there. It saddened him beyond his level of comfort.

Alex's people interacted, but Brian's heart wasn't in it. He recognised a common expression of mindless indifference in everyone. They were all living in the moment, a hot meal and somewhere to sit. They'd mostly lost the ability to communicate, and it had a very negative affect on Brian. He wished he hadn't come.

'You're doing a wonderful job here, Alex, and you have a special gift. There's no way I could do what you're doing. It's been great to meet some of them, but I have to get back home and give Sally a bit of a break from the kids.' And he was gone.

'Whose your snooty friend, Reverend?' they asked Alex when Brian had gone.

'Is he a bishop or something?' asked another.

Alex found himself defending Brian as a colleague working in a different area of ministry, but they weren't really interested in who he was. He just didn't fit in their world.

Brian was able to see the dependency Alex's congregation had on him, but not how he was dependent upon Brian.

Before entering the church, Alex had always been troubled by what might happen to him without Brian's guidance. It had become an important part of his existence. He often recalled his teenage years, during which he'd sought Brian's words of wisdom; and here he was now, in the church, with all those years behind him and the same dependency, not from a religious perspective but simply a worldly perspective. He was never able to organise his thoughts of how he would cope if Brian hadn't been there to advise him, to consult and guide him through his anxieties. Alex continually worried about his future.

When Alex first mentioned the issue of fringe people when they were curates, Brian had advised him to go with the flow, follow his heart, take each day as it came. One of the things he remembered giving comfort was Brian's comment, 'Don't worry about tomorrow. There's nothing you can achieve by worrying. Just deal with today.' Brian even quoted a Bible verse in which Jesus had said exactly the same thing.

Alex had written it down, Matthew Chapter 6:Verse 34. 'Do not worry about tomorrow, for tomorrow will worry about itself. Each day has enough trouble of its own.'

Alex was beginning to think this Jesus bloke knew a thing or two, because Alex certainly had his own problems day by day. Even though he didn't understand what *pastoral care* meant, the bishop had complimented Alex on his ministry. In his daily routine, Alex could only handle one issue at a time.

When the job in hand was completed, he could move on to the next issue. If the day had three or four issues to address, he'd worry about them to the exclusion of even starting on the first issue, because he put all his effort into worry. He just couldn't get his mind around progressive thinking to approach each issue by setting priorities. As a consequence, he'd often end his day having done nothing! Worry could completely overpower him at times, except whatever he didn't do, he always fed his street people. At the end of the day, when they were bedded down for the night, he'd reflect in the quiet of his own space. *Is there something I should be doing? Is there something I've forgotten to do today?*

Poor Alex, life was so complicated!

He jumped as his cell phone rang. The screen showed a blocked number, but he knew who it was; she often called about this time of day. He accepted the call. 'How about three thirty this afternoon?'

'See you there,' Alex said as he forgot all his inhibitions. Sex with her was the highlight of his week, and he knew he had to get into the shower and freshen up.

CHAPTER FORTY-TWO

CHARLES CONTINUED HIS middle-of-the-road attitude in ministry, even to the point of perfecting the middle road. His curacy had been uneventful. He didn't shine in any particular area, and consequently, he'd experienced a number of unsuccessful interviews with church councils for senior minister posts.

What came naturally to Brian was organising, public speaking, committee work, etc. Alex's natural motivation was instinctive—to serve the needy (second place, of course, to serving the dean's wife). They'd all entered the church for the same wrong reasons, but their characters had led them in totally different directions. Charles's character as Mr Average led him absolutely nowhere, which made him the odd man out. Logic would have made Alex the odd man out.

The highlight of Charles's week was also a romp in bed with the dean's wife. She continued to grow in her sexual demands. As usual, Charles didn't complain.

'Are you enjoying our sex?' she asked one day.

'Absolutely, I look forward to it more and more each week. I think you've taught me a great deal,' he said.

His response shocked her because she hadn't realised he'd recognised her hidden intent, but clearly Charles had picked up on this part of their relationship. It was easy for Charles to comply, and like his two colleagues, he wasn't complaining.

He'd struggled in his ministry, mainly because he wasn't even trying to understand what he was doing. Neither Brian nor Alex tried to understand either. They did what was expected, even though they were each very different personalities. It wasn't beyond Charles's ability or even his imagination. But it required a plan and a commitment to achieve, and he had neither. Apart from his sexual activities with the dean's wife, he was living outside his comfort zone. He needed to continually remind himself the church objective was an easy life with provisions such as the house, the regular wage, and the absence of stress to achieve in competition with others. But he felt his life was empty.

It was interesting, therefore, when they next met socially at the Pig and Whistle. Both Alex and Charles shared their thoughts about what they thought was missing in their lives.

A church-renewal person might have said, 'What's missing in your lives is the Holy Spirit.' But they weren't into renewal, which was bringing something back considered to have been lost. These guys hadn't lost anything!

Brian was a secular man, so his advice offered a worldly solution.

CHAPTER FORTY-THREE

B RIAN'S ADVICE WAS provocative. 'What you both need is a wife and family.'

'Another one of your brilliant ideas,' said Alex. 'I don't think so.'

Charles was more inclined towards the suggestion. 'Where would I look? My old hunting grounds have the wrong type of girls in circulation. There's no way I would marry any of them.'

Alex had a different reaction but held his comment.

'I would have thought the most likely place would be your own church,' said Brian. 'I'll bet there are several likely young ladies looking in your direction already. Try the grapevine, and let them know you're on the market.'

'What, put a notice up on the church notice board?' said Charles. '"Wanted, a wife for the curate. Must be good in bed."'

Alex thought it was not only a good idea but also a serious suggestion; however, he was learning to keep his mouth shut. *Maybe he wasn't serious—in which case, if I say anything, I'll put my foot in it again.*

'Seriously,' said Brian. 'Mention it in passing to your senior minister. Don't make a big deal about it. I'm sure you'll soon get propositioned. I learnt all about the grapevine at Heddingtons. It's extremely effective— more so if you don't start the grapevine chatter yourself, so if someone responds and they're not a person you fancy, you can always deny any knowledge of it, dismissing it as rumour.'

So Charles activated the grapevine as suggested and waited. The first came as an invitation to dinner with a middle-aged couple in his congregation. They had a daughter of appropriate age. Seemingly, she wasn't a party girl and had no social life other than church. Angela was shy and didn't appear to be a willing participant in the underlying purpose for the dinner. It was rather embarrassing for all concerned.

'Thank you for coming and spending some social time with us, Charles. This is our daughter, Angela.'

She responded with a handshake and was clearly embarrassed. Her communication was limited. 'Hello' squeaked out, and she then clammed up into silence.

'Do you have any family?' Angela's mother enquired, stopping marginally close to asking him if he was married. She knew he wasn't but wanted to raise the issue in her less-than-subtle way. The meal continued in silence, and Charles withdrew as soon as politeness allowed.

Charles bumped into Angela after the Sunday service and apologised for her parents' manner of trying to marry her off. She was a totally different person away from her parents, and they got on rather well. The difference between Angela and all the girls he'd been out with before had a significant impact upon him. If Charles was Mr Average, Angela was Miss Average. She had absolutely no redeeming features in figure or dress sense, but Charles enjoyed her company. She made him laugh; she spoke intelligently on any subject. They liked the same style of music, and it wasn't long before they were going out on dates together.

Married clergy were more acceptable at interviews for senior minister positions, especially if they had children. Charles very quickly announced his intent to marry Angela, a name none of his friends recognised because she was not from the circuit of girls he used to date. She was a pleasant enough girl, but both Alex and Brian wondered about his choice. She was not as tall as Charles, was slim, had boyish short brown hair, was flat-chested, and had hardly any hips. She didn't wear make-up and displayed minimal outward signs of femininity.

'Have you met Charles's fiancé?' Alex asked Brian before Charles arrived at the pub.

'Yes,' said Brian. 'She's a very pleasant girl, and I think he's made a wise choice. Her name is Angela, and she's a member of Charles's congregation, so I guess she's a Christian.'

'It's a good job her name isn't Jane,' said Alex. 'She's so plain. When I think of all the girls he'd dated—blondes, brunettes, redheads, tall, shapely, and sexy . . . I was always very jealous. But Angela?'

Charles joined them, and he was expecting comments about Angela other than anything complimentary. 'I know she wouldn't win any beauty competitions,' said Charles. 'But she makes me laugh, she's great company, and we talk a lot about all sorts of things. She never pretends to be anyone other than her natural self. All those girls I used to date were actresses, social butterflies. Angela is a real person, and I'm very happy she's agreed to marry me.'

Your choice, thought Alex, whose considerations were singularly how she'd perform in bed, and he'd grave doubts for Charles in that department.

Brian chipped in, 'Well, I think you're very lucky to have found each other and to have a soul mate. It's great to have a friend as well as a wife.' Brian was always ready to encourage.

CHAPTER FORTY-FOUR

T HE DEAN HADN'T been away for a while due to a building project he was managing at the cathedral. This was a major responsibility for any dean to administrate. It was a twelve-month project, which so far had taken eighteen months with associated cost overrun. He was clearly stressed, and the worldly management was beyond his ability.

'Brian, I'd like you to come and help me with the building project at the cathedral. I'm sure your architectural experiences will be invaluable. As you know, I'm due to go overseas in a couple of weeks, and it won't nearly be finished by then.'

'Of course,' said Brian. How could he refuse?

The expenditure overrun was in the hundreds of thousands of dollars, and the dean's stress level was overwhelming him. The cathedral owned real estate assets, and the dean and Brian decided to liquidate these assets to pay off the debt. It was the only solution they were able to come up with, and they were too embarrassed to ask advice from professionals.

They'd resolved the financial problem. Now Brian could deal with practical completion.

The threesome looked forward to the dean's impending trip for obvious personal reasons of their sexual gratification with the dean's wife. It was not long after the dean's departure that she was on the phone.

Invitations had become so routine; all she said now was the time. The venue and the reason for the invitation required no dialogue. Brian was pleased to return to his happy state of servicing the dean's wife, fulfilling both their desires.

Even though by this stage all three were aware they'd each had sex with the dean's wife, they'd no idea when the others were invited. She felt able to make invitations as frequently as her libido called.

The three clergy did, however, draw a plausible conclusion from the increased frequency of their invitations. She would have no time to participate in sexual activity with anyone else. So much so they discarded the archbishop as an ongoing participant. Having now met the bishop, Alex convinced his two friends the bishop was not a participant either. Well, they never really thought he was.

'And remember,' said Alex one day at the pub, 'he wasn't on page B in the little blue book!'

They all laughed, for different reasons, and Alex felt a glow of acceptance since he'd actually made a joke they found funny.

CHAPTER FORTY-FIVE

C HARLES CAME BACK from the bar with the second round of beers.

'Do you realise we've been in ministry for nearly two years?' said Charles as he sipped his beer.

'We've changed quite a lot in two years,' added Brian. 'But the good old Pig and Whistle never changes.'

'What's up, Alex? Lost your tongue all of a sudden?'

'Just enjoying a quiet drink. Something wrong with that?'

'OK, don't get snappy. You had a bad day?'

'No, I'm just thinking about stuff. Charles is now married. Brian's been married for a few years. I'm feeling a bit of a wallflower. Brian is getting all the exposure, like he's on TV next week, being interviewed by a bossy female journalist. Then he's on a TV quiz game. He's getting more exposure than the prime minister.'

'You jealous then?' asked Brian. 'I can get you on TV if you want, just give me the word.'

'No way! I wouldn't go on TV even if they paid me,' said Alex. 'Do they pay you, by the way?'

Brian decided not to answer; it was his business. Brian had been developing his career as a high-profile senior minister, seen throughout the diocese and the media as the go-to person regarding any issue remotely involving the need of a church voice. The church supported his TV appearances in the knowledge it was better to have a voice than to be silent, an all-too-often criticism of the church.

Alex withdrew into himself as Charles and Brian enjoyed a chat. They were at their usual table away from listening ears. Brian was itching to share his latest news with his two friends.

'I've been working on a plan to get spiritual leaders together from all faiths. The police are having a hard time with drugs, wayward youth, and violence in the streets, so I've invited different church leaders along to talk about what we might do.'

Alex appeared not to have been listening but decided to enter the discussion. 'So what do you think you can do that hasn't been tried already?'

'You're missing the point, Alex. I'm not trying to come up with something new. The point is, it will show the public the church cares. More particularly *our* church cares enough to try. The others aren't trying anything.'

Alex was now involved at his level of his misunderstanding. 'So how will anyone know you and these other denominations talked about it?'

Brian was getting a little exasperated. 'It's not rocket science. It's all about timing. There's no point in shining a spotlight on children's TV or early morning TV. Producers position programmes to attract targeted age groups. I don't do it, TV programmers do it.'

'That's not what I meant,' said Alex. 'How will you get Hindu, Muslim, Buddhists, and Christians all to come and talk to you?'

'Because my strategy is to make the whole thing public before I invite them to appear, so they'd be too embarrassed not to appear. If they didn't accept my invitation, the public would think they didn't care or didn't want to contribute to the solution and instead were part of the problem,' explained Brian.

'Sounds like a circus to me,' said Alex.

'Now you're getting it,' said Brian. 'It will be a circus. A showtime event organised and planned by our church. The viewing public will see we are being proactive towards these social issues and are actually trying to doing something.'

'But you're not doing anything,' said Alex. 'You're just talking.'

'TV is entertainment,' said Brian. 'This will be a reality TV show, attracting a thinking audience because it will be aired at prime time—seven thirty or eight o'clock p.m.' Brian reflected, *The dean couldn't fail to be impressed with my brilliant idea.*

Charles decided to voice his opinion. 'So you could have invited all these spiritual leaders and police to a meeting behind closed doors.'

'Yes, of course,' said Brian. 'But nobody would ever know who turned up. Nobody would know who said what. Even if we invited the press, they would report what they thought was relevant. This way they will be identified within their faith, and everything they say will be on the public record.'

'Still doesn't mean anything will happen' was to be Alex's last word on the subject. 'Who's for another beer?'

Even before Brian had invited the spiritual leaders, he'd approached the media and the story of him actually doing something the police were unable to do. It captured the attention of newspaper and magazine journalists. They reported the church was actually doing something practical instead of political debate telling everybody about the shortfall in funding. In reality, it was not the church introducing a proactive suggestion, it was Brian. *To me be the glory. Great things I have done!* Brian thought.

'Who will chair the meeting?' Charles wanted to know.

'Me, of course. It's my idea, and I'll invite each leader to make comment. It will be a bit like having a church group meeting, I won't actually say anything other than lead others up the garden path.'

'What about reporters and journalists who will want to ask questions?' Alex said to try and throw cold water on the whole thing.

'I won't let them anywhere near the TV studio, or it will get out of hand. I'll deal with them afterwards in private interviews. I've got contacts in TV, and it's time to call in a few favours.'

This was a hot topic. Pride was written all over the exercise, except there was no plan to actually do anything. It was just a talkfest with Brian as the leader getting wide public exposure. Before the TV programme was even advertised, radio talk shows were talking about it on air. Brian gave his first series of radio interviews to the Christian Broadcasting channel 7WGH with Anthony Briar, one of his useful contacts on the board of trustees.

There was no limit to the pride Brian could heap upon himself, positioned as he was in the most prestigious parish in the diocese— St Aiden's. He was also known to be successful because the parish financial books always balanced, with never a bad debt. The retail outlets continued to contribute significantly towards parish income, part of which was consolidated into the diocese general account.

How could anyone inside or outside the church consider him other than the pride of the diocese? He'd earned the characteristic of being very successful by his peers as well as his superiors, all of whom supported the public perception that it wouldn't be long before he took the next step up the ecclesiastical ladder. This was also perceived to have followed a very successful career as an architect which he'd sacrificed some years before.

CHAPTER FORTY-SIX

THE HOUSE BRIAN was offered when he was appointed senior minister fell short of what he'd expected for such a prominent senior posting. He persuaded the church council to upgrade the house in keeping with his expectations. To some extent, these expectations reflected new regulations the diocese implied were appropriate for senior ministers, notwithstanding the house had accommodated its previous senior minister and his family very comfortably for many years.

Because Brian's architectural skills were non-existent, he hired a consultant to bring his plans to fulfilment. His justification was based on his workload preventing dedicated time to spend time on such a mundane project. Of course, he'd a few ideas he was able to articulate, as did Sally, who by now had become the perfect clergyman's housewife and mother to his two children.

Her ideas focused mainly upon the kitchen and bathrooms, which were the most expensive rooms in any refit. Sally didn't just want a bathroom; she wanted an en suite bathroom.

It was interesting how the church council approved the budget for this work, considering the cost exceeded the total median house price in the area. It also exceeded the most expensive house in the area. After all, they'd started with a very acceptable house in the first place.

One part of the refit addressed Brian's study, which had to have independent access with its own front door. Previous access subjected the family to an unacceptable infringement on their privacy. If ever he was to have a guest at home, he decided his furniture should at least match the quality and comfort of his Catholic friend Carlos. He decided not to install a cocktail cabinet, because it could raise a few ecclesiastical eyebrows. In any event, he normally met guests in his church office—it was much less comfortable, and they wouldn't stay too long. The house refurbishment project ended up as a five-bedroom rectory having two spare bedrooms. Sally had an idea, which she quickly put to Brian.

'Now we have a couple of spare bedrooms, we'll need a housekeeper to do some cleaning. The house is far too big for me to handle on my own with two children and all. I could help financially by renting the two spare rooms to Japanese students. The English school across the road is always looking for local accommodation. What do you think?'

Offsetting any costs for housekeeping with income from students influenced Brian's response. 'OK, darling, I'll leave it to you. I don't need to be involved in anything to do with housekeeping.'

Having done her research, Sally discovered overseas parents not only paid school fees but also accommodation. Payments were made by EFT (electronic funds transfer) directly into the bank; all she had to do was provide EFT data to the English school, and the money would roll in. The rectory was within a short walking distance from the English school, and a word to the principal booked the two spare rooms immediately. Sally took advice from the principal and charged the going rate of $400 per student per week.

It was not long before Sally learnt students didn't expect to have their own bedroom and accommodation was more often backpacker style, providing shared rooms. Sally approached Brian with her developing plan.

'Darling, I've been told students normally share a bedroom, so with the money I've earned so far, I'm going to buy some bunk beds. This means I can accommodate four students in each room. They're out at school all day. They eat out, so there's nothing for me to do other than get the housekeeper to change the sheets and occasionally vacuum the carpets.'

Brian was only half listening and agreed. 'So long as the money doesn't come out of parish funds, I can't see any problem.'

Sally's little business blossomed. If a student left, there was always a waiting list to immediately take up the vacancy. Brian didn't do the math, but Sally had it all worked out before she bought the new bunk beds. She even sold the two single beds because they were almost new. Her little business started at $400 a week for two students but had grown into eight students at $400 a week. She created income of $166,400 a year. Not bad pocket money, and nothing to do with the diocese or any financial accountability to the church. Sally justified the legality by declaring her income and paying tax. As a result, she felt completely within her rights not to mention this to the church—nothing to do with them.

'Well done, Sally, I'm proud of you,' said Brian. 'This extra money will enable us to take the children to the snowfields for a skiing holiday. It would be uncomfortable driving there in our little car. Why don't we buy a Land Cruiser four-wheel drive?' It was something beyond their means without Sally's contribution.

They'd both settled into the sort of comfortable lifestyle Brian had always expected, and all he'd done was to exploit his personal skills. Sally had contributed significantly, and her little scheme for students contributed more than double Brian's stipend.

Both Sally and Brian developed their own lifestyle economies having no accountability to the church. Apart from Sally's little business, Brian earned fees at speaking engagements, which they called love offerings. They also paid for his various TV appearances, which if ever repeated generated royalties. Brian needed an agent to look after his various speaking engagements and TV appearances.

The agent insulated Brian from having to negotiate fees. Both he and Sally were using their skills as well as church property and time for personal gain. Sally never got involved in any church activities other than the occasional appearance at a Sunday service. Well, she had the children to look after.

CHAPTER FORTY-SEVEN

THERE WERE TWO activities in Alex's life. One was his sexual activity with the dean's wife, and for him at least, it dominated his thoughts when he wasn't actively doing anything else. The other was serving his congregation in his unique way.

Since ordination, he'd kept his sexual encounters limited to the dean's wife. Although he was unable to operate a laptop or computer, he would be lost without his cell phone. She would call and invite him to the motel. He'd developed a habit of continually looking at his cell phone to see if he'd missed her call. He could've performed for her every day, but she only called when she wanted sex, which might be only a couple of times a week. He never complained.

His phone vibrated in his pocket.

'Are you available this afternoon, four o'clock p.m.?' she said.

As he tried to make his reply, his fingers kept touching the wrong buttons, and he was in danger of cutting her off. He never said no, but he could never simply say yes. He was muddled in preparation of speaking; the cell phone was no different.

He arrived at the motel, looking in every direction for anyone who might be watching. It was raining, but he didn't notice. He strolled to the motel door and gently knocked. He was familiar with the motel, having been there several times already, and he arrived late even though he'd been ready for a couple of hours.

Alex was ready to go as soon as he arrived, and she had no success slowing him down sufficiently to gain control. He was obviously much stronger than her, and apart from her efforts to teach, she was forced to go at his speed.

'Next time, Alex, I'll show you some of the techniques of lovemaking.'

'Why, wasn't I any good?'

'Of course, you are. I'm just trying to share some of the finer points of sex so we can enjoy it even more.'

Alex was confused. Sex was sex, and enjoyment was enjoyment—what more was there to know? He was not only unaware of any finer points, he didn't want to know. His insecurity had taken a body blow, but discussion was not worth the effort. She was almost thinking it was time to end the relationship. But he did have a contribution to make; she couldn't let him go. She knew the next time would be the same and was able to forgive his exuberance for the sheer immediacy of his lust. She reminded herself once again that he was different to the other two, and how boring it would be if they were all the same. She was completely unaware of his ADHD, but she was beginning to understand his behaviour was unchangeable.

It was at this time that Alex's ministry had taken a different direction from Brian's and Charles's. He was a gentle and generous soul and started providing more than food. The money had come from his own wage to start with, but the soup kitchen had grown beyond his ability to finance. The number of people to feed had grown significantly. It had been able to grow because money had been provided from an unknown source. He knew it wasn't from the church.

His reputation of reaching out to fringe people had been noticed by a senior politician who himself had been trained at a seminary for priesthood but hadn't taken his vows. The Christian politician directed funds in support of Alex's ministry from a government grant initiated for well-meaning services to society.

Alex might have considered himself a notional Christian or, more likely, not a Christian at all, having gone along with Brian's influence to enter the church all those years ago. However, even though he didn't know it, he was a more of an active Christian than many—if not most—clerics.

He wasn't conversant with the Bible so far as quoting chapter and verse. But he didn't hide behind biblical narrative in an effort to conceal the compassion he genuinely felt towards his congregation. If someone quoted a verse he recognised, he always doubted the relevance for it living in today's world. A contradiction of this was a passage someone had quoted from the book of James, because he recognised this in himself. He even thought that perhaps he might be a Christian after all.

The passage was James Chapter 1 Verse 19: 'Everyone should be quick to listen, slow to speak and slow to become angry.'

That's me, thought Alex, *although I'm not so sure about 'slow to become angry'.*

So Alex continued ministering in his unique way, reaching out to those disadvantaged by society and neglected by social services. Most of his congregation were living on the street; others were unable to keep themselves clean. It wasn't that they didn't want to keep clean. It was because they'd nowhere to shower, nowhere to wash their clothes. Alex provided a hot shower and towels. He didn't say they had to shower or even suggest they might need to shower; it was just another thing he provided, offered to one and all.

The sleeping arrangements, particularly in the winter, were still available in the heated meeting room where Alex had now put some camp beds to keep occupants off the floor. However he was suddenly confronted with a bureaucratic dilemma from the local council. He didn't realise he needed permission to use church property as a bed-and-breakfast facility any more than he had to comply with fire regulations. The council would only permit him to continue if he converted the premises to an acceptable level of compliance. This would mean application to the council with a DA (development application) drawing up plans to comply with building regulations. This was beyond Alex's ability, and he didn't understand why he needed to do it anyway.

There needed to be a certain number of toilets dependent upon how many beds, he'd have to segregate men from women . . . it went on and on. It was too much for Alex to cope with and unlikely to gain approval anyway—just something else for him to worry about.

CHAPTER FORTY-EIGHT

A LEX'S UNDERSTANDING OF social services was that they didn't provide facilities for these people and were happy for them to live on the street, to use the public toilets having no hot water or showers, and to be moved on by police when people complained. They didn't provide facilities like affordable meals and denied Alex from providing services free of charge.

He consulted his friends.

'This is stupid. The council won't provide any help, and now they want to stop me from doing it. What's the sense in that?'

'This is the way things are done—this is the real world in which we live,' said Charles. 'If you ever look for logic or try to understand, you'll get nowhere,' Brian added.

They had no solution of course, not even Brian. Alex wondered again about the gifts of the Spirit and asked his two friends how he might access these gifts. Brian and Charles weren't far short of being atheists although their thoughts had drifted across passages of scripture they'd wondered about.

'My understanding', said Brian, 'is that these gifts were just for apostolic times and are no longer available to the church. At least that's what we were taught at theology college.'

Charles had no words of wisdom on the subject, and the issue had never been mentioned in his church. He did remember they spoke words from the service of Holy Communion mentioning the Holy Spirit by name, just a throwaway line.

'I've never had any questions asked in my church about the Holy Spirit,' said Charles. 'It seems to be a no-brainer.'

This seemed to be one of those subjects many mainstream churches never spoke about. It fell in the 'too hard' basket.

Alex knew there was a celebration or festival day in the church calendar—something to do with Pentecost, when there was supposed to have been a great witness of the Spirit—but, of course, that was a long time ago.

'It's just a festival now in memory of the event so it's no longer relevant,' Brian concluded.

Charles realised Alex had a problem but didn't understand why he wanted to know about the gifts of the Spirit. Alex was aware many problems in his ministry had been mysteriously resolved. He certainly hadn't resolved them himself. He was revisiting his belief in God, who he believed was guiding him as well as meeting the needs of those he was serving. He was just trying to understand the source of help, especially if it was coming through the ministry of the Holy Spirit as gifts. As usual, he was unable to explain this to his friends.

He could see the gift of wisdom in Charles's choice of Angela. He could see the gift of knowledge in Brian, who always knew what to say in any situation. However, his conscience told him it also could've been Charles's luck and Brian's worldly experience. *Well, Brian had been an architect. Maybe I could have the gift of tongues, whatever that is, or some other hidden gift. But what's the point of having it if I don't know what it is or how to use it?* Alex thought.

He'd become more convinced someone was helping him, blessing him. It couldn't be his bishop because he'd only met him once. Neither could it be his archbishop because he'd never met him other than at his ordination and there were several others priested at the same time. Of course, he'd been blissfully unaware Brian had been lobbying on his behalf, although it had nothing to do with helping Alex—it was more about helping Brian.

Alex decided to take a major step outside his comfort zone and seek counsel with his bishop. Having made the appointment, he worried about what he would say as well as what the bishop would think of his question. It was simply his insecurity rising up in his mind, and it wouldn't have been so bad if the appointment had been in a day or so, but it was three weeks away—plenty of time to worry! It was unusual to get an appointment as quickly as three weeks because the bishop's diary was always full. *Plenty of time to cancel the meeting,* he thought as he worried about it day after day.

He picked up his cell phone and called the bishop's office, but before the secretary answered, he hung up. *What shall I say if she asks, 'Why do you want to cancel?'* He couldn't think of a reason that sounded plausible. Nobody seemed to want to talk about the Holy Spirit.

His appointment was suddenly upon him, and he could do no more than attend, having no idea what he would say or how he would articulate his problem. The bishop was a short overweight man. His bushy eyebrows looked as if they were wings on an airplane. They almost took off as they rose and fell beneath his shiny bald head as his expressions changed from surprise to doubt. His eyes were small in comparison to the rest of his face, unusually close together, and penetrated Alex as he made eye contact. They squinted as if he were trying to see through a haze of smoke, except there was no smoke.

Despite what Alex had considered would be an intimidating meeting, it went remarkably well at the beginning, and he'd hardly needed to say a word.

'I'm delighted to meet you, Alex. I've heard glowing reports of your ministry. If only we had a few more like you, my job would be so much easier.'

Job? thought Alex. *I didn't think you worked. You just sit behind a desk and talk to people.*

As the bishop heaped praise on him, he wondered how the man knew, because the bishop had never attended his soup kitchen or any of his services. Maybe the bishop has some of that Holy Spirit stuff and was able to have insight into things happening around the diocese.

Eventually, the bishop asked, 'Well, Alex, how can I help you?'

Then it just spilled out. 'I'm very grateful to those who've contributed financially to meet the needs of my parishioners, but the local council have threatened closure unless I comply with heaps of regulations. I just want to use my church for the benefit of these disadvantaged people.'

That suppressed the bishop's enthusiasm, and after a long silence, he said, 'Leave it with me, Alex. I'll see what I can do.'

While I'm here, he thought. And in a sudden rush of confidence, Alex raised the issue of the gifts of the Spirit. 'Can you tell me about the gifts of the Spirit?'

In Alex's naivety, he didn't realise the answer one gets depends upon the question one asks.

'Yes, of course, Alex,' said the bishop, and he referred Alex to the Bible, 1 Corinthians, starting at verse 12 and quoting, 'There are different kinds of gifts, but the same Spirit. There are different kinds of service but the same Lord. There are different kinds of working, but the same God works all of them in all men. Now in each one the manifestation of the Spirit is given for the common good. To one there is given through the Spirit the message of wisdom, to another the message of knowledge, by means of the same Spirit. . . .'

Alex waited patiently for enlightenment as he looked out of the window, up at the ceiling, down at his feet. The bishop intensified his penetrating look at Alex across the desk. The biblical narrative appeared to be the extent of the bishop's knowledge and answer on the subject.

Alex knew he could have looked that up in the Bible himself. He was hoping to get some insight into how he would go about getting a gift of the Spirit and using it. He sat quietly in front of the bishop, wondering if there was more to be said. But the bishop's silence had gone on too long, and he stood and extended his hand.

'Thank you so much for coming, Alex. It's so good to meet a servant of God who is working in the community. Please come and see me again whenever you like, and I'll get to work on your problem with council.'

Alex felt relieved he'd passed his burden over to his bishop, even though he'd learnt nothing about the gifts of the Spirit. In the meantime, he would continue to accommodate his parishioners and feed them in his soup kitchen.

Problem solved without Brian, thought Alex.

After about six months, he'd received no communication from his bishop or from the local council, so he thought either the bishop had been successful sorting it out so that either council or the Holy Spirit had intervened. It was almost a year later that he received the notice of closure from the council, and his heart sank. His thoughts immediately retreated into doubt of the Holy Spirit, as he reflected upon his visit to the bishop. *All a waste of time. I need to talk to Brian.*

When they caught up in the pub, Charles reacted quite strongly to the news of council threatening closure and suggested Alex contact a TV station with the story. 'The church is doing something practical,' said Charles. 'Well, at least Alex is, and the council is knocking a good bloke down.'

Brian shared something he'd noticed in his local park, maintained by the same council. 'There's a picnic shelter close to a BBQ. Some homeless people sleep out overnight, especially if it's raining. The council's solution was to board it up and stick a notice outside saying "This shelter is temporarily closed for refurbishment". It had been reported in the local newspaper that it might take a week or so to paint, even though it hadn't needed painting, yet it's still boarded up after six months. Council workers haven't been near the place. Clearly it was an underhanded way of dealing with a problem too hard to confront. Boarding it up achieved the required result, preventing homeless people taking shelter at night.'

'Very interesting,' said Alex. 'But what's that got to do with what I'm talking about?'

'It's another example of bureaucracy not working for the needs of the people,' said Brian. 'I'll approach my friends at the commercial TV station where I'm well known. I'm sure they'll agree to run a story about Alex's wonderful ministry meeting the needs of homeless people while the council does nothing. Police just move them on, where to they don't care. We could also use the story about the boarded-up shelter to reinforce the bureaucratic attitude towards those less able to provide for themselves.' Brian was winding up with enthusiasm.

As it turned out, the programme never went to air because various parties had got together and put pressure on the TV station, threatening to withdraw advertising revenue if they proceeded. It wouldn't be good for the council, and it was suggested that if Alex were allowed to continue by simply ignoring the council's notice of closure, the TV programme would be cancelled.

Charles shared an opinion. 'It would've been good for the church to be seen as an institution reaching out to these people, not that I could do it in my parish for obvious reasons.'

Brian wasn't prepared to cancel, however, and agreed only to shelve the TV programme just in case he'd ever need to resurrect it for future negotiation.

And so Alex's ministry carried on, Brian storing the information for future recall, Charles marking time and enjoying the fruits of his chosen employer, and Alex reinvigorated by having offloaded his burden once again to Brian. The bishop had obviously failed Alex, but what matter—Brian had come to the rescue again.

CHAPTER FORTY-NINE

THE DEAN WAS about to embark on what everyone thought might be his last overseas speaking tour as retirement age closed in. The three clergymen and, more importantly, the dean's wife, needed to reacquaint their relationships. She didn't invite them in any particular order other than what appeared to reflect a completely random selection. Doubtless, there were reasons so far as she was concerned, but as the threesome compared their respective sexual schedules, they concluded the selection process was completely random.

Brian and Charles's encounters had developed into routine transgressions, no longer sexual anticipation—the lead up to knocking on the door, even the excitement as they entered the motel. Sex was fulfilling in a singularly satisfying way, and each wondered if they would even get another invitation. Such was the inevitable activity of sex without love; it had a fairly short shelf life.

Alex, on the other hand, was always eager to perform, doubtless because he'd not married and had limited access to anyone willing to participate in fulfilling his sexual appetite. During their time of sharing, it became evident Alex was performing in the ratio of two-to-one compared with his two friends. There was no jealousy. It was the way of the world, and the church didn't influence their activities with the dean's wife. It was justified at a personal level, as there was need—and in Alex's case, greed.

For some reason, the transgressions of the dean's wife weren't as much a secret as she'd thought. The dean had long since come to terms with the reality his wife had a much more active appetite for things of the flesh heterosexually. The significance of this wasn't so much the dean's diverse sexual appetite but more because it freed them both of marital restraint. Accordingly, he had encouraged the extramarital activity—at least with Brian—provided she was discreet. So it suited all interested parties: the threesome, the dean, but mostly, the dean's wife.

Her libido had not diminished during her advancing years and had, in fact, grown during her association with the three young clergymen. They were not to know the operative word was *young*, and she found it irresistible to engage with inexperienced young men. She reflected on their progress and how different they'd been when she'd first seduced them. The gap between her experience and their inexperience was great, which she kept reminding herself was where the pleasure had been spawned. She'd developed what she liked to think of as a gentlemen's behaviour, which was all about how her suitors should approach the fairer sex, which may have been purely social or in a more intimate way. Irrespective, she was a critique of men's behaviour towards women. It was yet another example of recognising other people's faults without recognising her own. Her criticism of men with whom she'd associated, apart from the three current beaus, were they were only interested in self-gratification, and yet this was her primary objective as a nymphomaniac.

She was doing this in a quasi-legitimate way, reflecting her self-justification because she was aware inexperienced young men had all the motivation and equipment but none of the etiquette or experience. She was also aware experimentation had already taken place with the younger generation, but not necessarily with experienced partners. It was much more likely their sexual experiences had been with young girls of a similar age.

CHAPTER FIFTY

WHEREAS THE DEAN'S wife had a number of attributes, she was completely naive when using budget motels for her clandestine purpose. Dan, a disreputable motel owner, had a camera set up in the room, providing his afternoon entertainment.

Nobody rented a room for an afternoon sleep, so he was aware why people rented a room at this time of day. It provided him with original pornographic material, and it was obvious she was entertaining more than one man, so the camera rolled on almost to full capacity. He was able to download from the camera, edit out the uninteresting parts, and file it as a stand-alone hard disc via his laptop.

Dan thought he'd every right to film what was going on in his premises. He justified himself as collecting evidence for the police, who might one day ask him to assist them with their enquiries. Of course, he had to review the footage from time to time to check content. It developed into a hobby of his deranged mind.

His new client had provided him with a completely new experience; it was a bit like watching a sex school. He watched intently as each young man was guided towards sensitive touching spots, but he wasn't as much interested in that, as was his motivation of feral lust. With his insatiable sexual appetite, he decided it was time to develop the relationship in a more practical way.

Dan knocked on her door after the third young man had left one afternoon. 'Hi there, I'm aware of what you're doing with these young men and thought you'd like to have a more experienced and adult sexual experience.'

Not surprisingly, her reaction was shock. 'No, thank you,' she said. 'I like to choose the partners I have sex with.' She tried not to antagonise him and politely thought she could close the matter by saying, 'Thank you, but no, thank you.'

Dan put his foot in the door, and she was not strong enough to overpower him as he pushed into the room.

'Perhaps I didn't make myself clear,' said Dan. 'It wasn't so much a request I was making, and you have to understand—I know what you're doing, and perhaps you don't want this to be made public. I have you on camera. I'm sure your husband would be very interested to see what you get up to during the afternoon.'

Dan was enjoying this. 'I see you open the door, wearing that flimsy negligee, clearly a willing and compliant partner. You're clearly in control and seduce these young men as an experienced woman. I like that! I'm sure you'd benefit having sex with an experienced man closer to your own age. I might even teach you something.'

In the heat of the moment, she had no answer; and in any event, he was in the room and she was on her own. She realised she'd been caught in the act with video recordings, and she wasn't going to escape without having sex with him.

How could I have been so stupid, coming back to the same motel week after week? she thought. 'OK, just this once,' she said.

Not if I have anything to do about it, thought Dan. *But we'll leave that to the next time.*

She'd no idea there was a camera hidden in the room, but that was not her focus at this time. After she thought he'd finished, she relaxed. But he withdrew, flipped her over, and took her from behind. This man was an animal. He was aggressive—even brutal—and in all her experience, which was quite considerable, she'd never come across anything like it before. His rigidity was relentless, his strength overpowering. He left her seriously bruised.

He thanked her, as if she might've enjoyed it as much as he had. Dan then just walked out and shut the door behind him. She showered but didn't feel clean. She decided to use a different motel each time in future, and this would be the last time she'd use Dan's motel. She'd always paid cash and never provided her name or address. As a consequence, she felt comfortable from any future imposition from this terrible man.

However, Dan wasn't going to let such an opportunity slip through his fingers easily, and to secure the prospect, he followed her home and got her address. *Nice home. Pretty exclusive area must be worth a bob or two.* Dan had no idea it was owned by the church, and even if he'd known it was called the deanery, it wouldn't have meant anything to him.

Because she'd never returned, Dan decided it was time to renew his acquaintance, and one day, he knocked on the front door of the deanery.

'Hi there. Remember me? I've come to give you a good time again. I hope it's convenient,' said Dan in a very matter of fact way.

She was horrified to see him standing in her space and felt threatened. She would not let him into her house; there was a chain lock to prevent the door opening fully.

'What do you want?' she said. 'I did what you wanted, so we're quits.'

'I don't think so,' said Dan. 'Like I told you, I have a camera in the motel room. You haven't quite paid my price yet, so I want you to come back to the same room tomorrow. Otherwise, I'll send a copy to your husband. Now I know your address. Perhaps a few other people might be interested to see what you get up to with those young men. Perhaps some of your neighbours?'

The thought of blackmail suddenly became a reality, and she needed a plan to deal with it so it wouldn't recur. She'd never been blackmailed before, and apart from the blackmail itself, the remembrance of his sexual onslaught was entirely repugnant. She closed the door, and he went away. The dean was still overseas, not that she would have approached him with her problem. These encounters were beyond the scope of the dean's latitude for extramarital activities. The obvious choice was Brian, who responded to her invitation, thinking it was for the usual purpose, even though the invitation had been to the deanery.

When he arrived, she was dressed quite differently, in very conservative slacks and jumper; she also seemed to have been crying. Brian immediately fell into his role of the advisor, the counsellor and the person everyone knew could solve any problem. However, he'd never had one like this before.

She didn't go into any detail or mention the brutality of Dan's attack on her body. She didn't mention the offending camera either, which had recorded Brian and his friends in such damming and conclusive evidence. She just described Dan as someone she used to know who had compromised her in blackmail.

'He's got some photos of me and threatens to send them to the dean.' She broke down in tears and was visibly shaken by the experience.

'I'll do anything I can to help, although I've no idea what to suggest at this stage.' Brian only knew one way of dealing with a blackmailer based on his knowledge watching TV. Because his identity was known, he thought it should be easier, but he wasn't about to suggest anything physical.

'What can we do?' she continued through her tears. It had now become a *we* instead of an *I* problem, but Brian didn't notice. Because she'd chosen the motel and implicated all three clergy, she didn't intimate the situation with Dan had anything to do with Brian, Charles, or Alex.

Brian's first thought was self-centred. He considered the effects of anything he might do which might affect his career. He'd become a tall poppy in the diocese as well as in the media. They would have a field day at his expense if it became known he was involved in blackmail. His second thought was of the dean's wife and how he might protect her. She'd surely express her appreciation in some tangible way.

'What type of man is this?' asked Brian.

'Frightful and aggressive, and a bit common.'

'What do you mean?' he queried.

'Well, he's not refined or what you would call a gentleman, nor is he in any way academic—not like us, Brian. Sort of low down the social ladder, if you know what I'm trying to say.' She was more than a bit of a snob.

Brian picked up on all the nuances, which justified his non-Christian thoughts. Perhaps his two friends could help scare him off with a bit of the 'physical'.

'I guess we need to deal with him,' said Brian without any detail. She took his hand and led him upstairs to the bedroom.

CHAPTER FIFTY-ONE

BRIAN WONDERED HOW to engage the help of his two friends regarding their common relationship with the dean's wife. They were all involved with her, and he decided they should at least be consulted. *Alex could probably deal with Dan on his own*, he thought, *and would be a great asset due to his physical strength*. He approached the prospect purely on the basis of meeting the need of the dean's wife. After all, without this problem, everything was going according to plan, not to mention the sexual activities he enjoyed en route.

The dean had more than hinted Brian would be appointed the next dean, even though at such a young age. Brian convinced himself he'd have to do something to help the dean's wife as well as his career. He thought long and hard how best to help her, but he kept coming up against his own inability to do anything on his own.

Discussion with the other two took a gentle approach to start with, Brian using his negotiating skills to the fullest. He tried to do this without suggesting anything physical. Even as clandestine clergymen, it would've been a bridge too far. He'd chatted around their combined relationship with the dean's wife, which had now been going on for a few years. They'd all benefited, and now she had a desperate need only they could fix. He was trying to get one of them to suggest foul play, to which he would obviously agree, but he didn't want to be the one to suggest it. Brian had embellished the story to position Dan in the worst possible light, even to justify the action they might eventually decide to take.

As they sat and chatted, often with long silences between suggestions, it eventually got around to how they might do it. Alex eventually suggested a few options. 'We could threaten him with physical violence unless he gave the photos back.'

But Charles saw the flaw. 'He could give some or all photos and keep copies. Dan could come back later and try again. The plan has no finality.'

They were all thinking murder, but nobody had suggested it yet.

Then, without actually putting it into words, 'How would we do it?' enquired Charles. 'None of us has a gun, so that's not an option. Nor do we own an appropriate knife, and the use of a kitchen knife would be too messy. We don't want to create a mess we can't clear up.'

'Maybe we should consult the dean's wife on her preferred method,' suggested Alex, but they ignored his suggestion. They were sure she didn't care about the methodology, just the outcome.

'We could always employ a contract killer, get someone else to do it for us,' suggested Charles.

'How could we afford to pay for it?' responded Brian. 'Those guys don't come cheap.'

Alex had a credible contribution. 'Apart from the fact we've no idea how to go about finding a contract killer, he might get caught and dob us in. Also, if the contract killer finds out we're clergymen, the fee will likely go up, and he will put the screws on us.'

The dialogue had moved well into the area of disposal of Dan, and without actually realising, they'd started to hatch a plan of murder.

'We've sort of decided the best way is without creating any mess,' said Charles.

'Yes, I agree,' said Brian. 'We're certainly not experts at this sort of thing, but there's no way we'll be able to dispose of a body, let alone clear up any mess.'

Alex was familiar with forensic TV shows and chipped in. 'It's not as simple as just clearing up any mess. It's more to do with clearing up any evidence we were ever at the scene of the crime. DNA and all the implications of unwittingly leaving something behind, even a single strand of hair. It's not just fingerprints they seem to be able to find with special equipment. I've seen them on TV. It's incredible what they find at a crime scene.'

On the negative side, they kicked around trying to make it look like suicide. 'We'd have to entice Dan away from his motel, since there were no beams or trees around his motel to make suicide by hanging appear credible.'

'The apparent suicide option could involve the dean's wife to entice him out of his motel,' suggested Alex, as if he'd not heard.

Their collective thoughts moved away from the motel to a remote place.

'But it would be too obvious for the dean's wife to invite him to a remote place where there just happened to be a tree. Dan's not stupid. If any transaction were to take place, he would want it to be at his motel,' Charles shared.

'Yes, I agree. Dan would be suspicious for sure if he was invited out of his motel and asked to bring the photos with him in exchange for anything, sex or money. We might as well ask him to bring a rope,' said Brian.

Alex was confused about the rope but eventually understood the sarcasm.

They'd all watched enough TV shows to know forensics eventually found suicide to have been murder, and the police would then be looking for evidence, suspects, and motive. They were comfortable nobody could directly link them to the motel or any association with the dean's wife other than being clergy within the diocese. A simple murder was agreed as the preferred option, and Dan's motel was as good a location as any.

So this was what it'd come to for three young clergymen so easily seduced into a minefield of worldly problems and all with their different plans for future gratification. Their humanistic reaction to deal with the problem of the dean's wife was not helped because their collars were back to front. Quite the opposite. They all remembered why and how they'd gotten into this lifestyle, and now someone they didn't even know threatened it. Poor Dan, he had to go—and the sooner the better.

CHAPTER FIFTY-TWO

THE DEVELOPING SITUATION had been playing in the mind of the dean's wife as she lay alone in bed. The dean was still overseas, and her thoughts became the subject of a very realistic dream. The dream started with the reality that Dan wanted her to visit him in his motel again. Her dream developed, and she was in no doubt what was going to happen; however, her anger and severe anxiety motivated her towards a plan to deal with him in a most severe manner. In her dream, she took a knife from her own kitchen—not a normal kitchen knife but what was known as a boning knife.

She'd never actually used it because it was one of those special chef's knives she'd bought as a birthday present for the dean. Goodness knows why—he never did any cooking! What scared her from ever using it was that it was so sharp. Apparently chemically sharpened (whatever that meant), the knife was made of some high-grade steel. The salesman had said if ever she felt it became dull or was damaged, she was to take it back, and he would resharpen it without charge. *And so he should. It cost enough money,* she thought.

She arrived at the motel reception at the appointed time, and Dan gave her the key to the room he liked to think of as his recording studio. She went down to the room to prepare herself for the onslaught. She placed the knife under the pillow and waited. Dan was as eager as the dean's wife was frightened. Dan first went to the toilet, and she checked to make sure the knife was well hidden. She was less than willing to Dan's advances but compliant, which was part of her plan. She waited on the bed, and he wasted no time in getting on with it. No foreplay for this guy.

Because at this time she was on her back, she was able to extend her arms above her head without attracting attention. She could feel the knife and carefully held it by the handle. Her plan was to thrust it into his back, confident the length of the blade wouldn't penetrate through his body and into her chest. Boning knives have a relatively short blade unlike carving knives, which were almost twice as long. As she stretched out her arms, it seemed to happen in slow motion. He was unable to see what she was doing as he was totally engrossed in his own lustful needs. When she'd grasped the knife in her right hand, she moved it around his back. Gripping it then with both hands, she plunged it into his back as hard as she could. She was surprised how easily the knife penetrated his flesh and was expecting to have had some resistance.

He arched his back in pain, not realising what had created it. She knew from watching murder films that people with knife wounds had a better chance of survival if the knife was left in situ. Removal allowed bleeding to take place at a faster rate. She withdrew the knife and plunged it in again. This time he collapsed on top of her and blood dripped from his mouth. He still had no idea what had befallen him.

As he looked into her eyes with abject amazement and surprise, she smiled at him and said, 'Goodbye, Dan, I can't say it's been good to know you.'

She removed the knife and rolled him off on to his back and noticed she was covered in blood. She showered and washed herself outwardly clean. Upon her return to the bedroom, she viewed the scene thinking, *What a mess, body fluids all over the place,* as her mind again recalled reruns of forensic movies. Then she awoke in a cold sweat, except she had an incredible feeling of satisfaction, almost orgasmic!

Next time they met, Alex seemed animated at the prospect of doing something illegal and suggested, 'Poison might be a good idea. No mess to clear up, and no problem of getting him out of his motel. We could turn up with the dose, get him drunk, and slip the stuff into his drink then find the photos. Just leave him there.'

'What if he doesn't drink?' said Charles. 'We can hardly suggest a chat drinking coffee and eating biscuits.'

'Surely the three of us could overpower him physically without all the cloak-and-dagger stuff,' said Charles. They were revisiting their plan in the effort of refinement so as to perform the perfect murder.

The final plan appeared the simplest and best. Alex would go to reception and ask for a room just for a couple of hours and would be sufficiently open about his motives, telling Dan he was having a woman in for a bit of fun.

'OK then, so it's settled,' said Brian. 'We'd better get it done before we come up with another plan. Otherwise, we'll spend all our time planning and not doing.'

'Tomorrow afternoon then,' said Charles. 'You got some rope?' he asked Alex. 'Don't go and buy some—that would create a trail of evidence. Either you've got some or you haven't.'

Alex understood and replied. 'I've got some, and I've had it for years. It's down in the back shed behind the church. We can tie him up, or I'll bring some sticky tape so we can strap him into a chair.'

Alex arrived at the motel and played his role as the guy wanting a room for a couple of hours to entertain a woman. When he got to his room, he suddenly realised their plan was flawed because there was no woman, so how were they going to get Dan down the room?

Good, thought Dan, *I'll get the camera rolling.* However his plan wasn't going to plan either because all he could see was Alex. He had no idea Dan planned to capture him in the act on film as his afternoon of entertainment. Having nothing else to do, Dan went down and knocked on the door. Alex covered brilliantly by saying she'd failed to turn up, even though he'd paid upfront. Perhaps it reflected a real-life situation Dan had actually experienced. It certainly convinced Dan.

'I'm going to have a drink, drown my sorrows. Would you like to join me?' Alex enquired.

It wasn't until Brian and Charles entered the room that Dan realised who they were as they quickly overpowered him and tied him up in a chair. They also gagged him so any cries for help wouldn't be heard. They discussed what to do next, and Charles took the initiative and put a rope around his neck and pulled it tight. Dan's eyes bulged and he fought against the restraints that held his hands and legs to the chair, but to no avail. Then Dan went limp. It was mission complete, so they took the rope off, removed his gag, and laid him on the bed.

'OK, that bit done and dusted. What next?' Alex was excited. Adrenaline was pumping, and they were each well out of their comfort zone.

'I'll go down to the office and get whatever I can find—photos, discs, laptop . . .' said Charles.

All of a sudden, Dan coughed and started to breathe again, gasping for air. They all pounced on him, and Alex got the rope around his neck again and pulled tighter this time and held it in place for ten minutes.

'Check his pulse?' Charles said, which of course they should've done the first time.

'Nothing! He's dead this time,' said Brian.

When Alex had checked into the motel, he'd given a false name, which Dan hadn't entered in a book anyway. He'd paid cash—no credit card to create a link back to him. Alex and Dan never got as far as having a drink, so there was no DNA left on drinking glasses.

The police would establish it was clearly murder, and the three clergymen felt confident there was no trail back to them either individually or collectively. Motive would be impossible to find, and the dean's wife was at arms' length to the entire debacle.

As they drove away, Brian quizzed Charles. 'Did you go through all the drawers in the office desk?'

'I virtually cleared the office. There was no time to look for specifics, so I just took everything. Laptop, backup hard drive, USB sticks, flash drives, DVDs. There were no hard-copy photographs so I guess he had everything stored electronically.'

'Good job you did that part,' said Alex. 'I wouldn't know a USB stick from a backup hard drive.'

'We all did our part,' said Brian. 'We've dealt with the dean's wife's problem in finality. Now let's smash up everything we've collected and dispose of it in a skip bin miles away.'

One thing they hadn't considered was that there may have been other motel guests who could have seen them. It was not as if they'd acted suspiciously outside the motel room, but anyone could have come into the reception area and been a witness to their presence. However they were lucky, and the unpopular motel had no other customers that afternoon.

They drove to the dean's house and told the dean's wife Dan would no longer be a problem.

'We've trashed all the records we found in his office such as his laptop and hard discs. There were no photos, and we're as sure as we can be we took and destroyed any records.' Brian was pleased to take credit for all the activities of the afternoon.

They stopped short of saying they'd murdered Dan, and their satisfaction of bringing finality to the situation was all the dean's wife needed to know.

'I think it would be a good idea if we had alibis,' said Brian.

'What on earth for? We've had no connection with Dan or his motel.' This made Alex nervous. They decided it was better to be safe than sorry. He could rely upon his congregation to back him up by confirming he'd been at the soup kitchen all afternoon, cooking. Every member of his congregation hated the police, who did nothing but move them on, and they would say whatever Alex wanted them to say for their beloved reverend.

Brian and Charles hatched a story they'd been at the dean's house all afternoon, preparing for a Bible study group later in the evening, and the dean's wife would confirm their story. They didn't think they would need an alibi. But this was what happened in the movies, so there was no harm in having a plan.

CHAPTER FIFTY-THREE

T HE NEXT DAY, they were surprised when a detective knocked on the door of the rectories of Brian, Charles, and Alex, inviting them to attend an interview at the local police station. The dialogue was the same, probably words rehearsed from the police manual.

'Good morning, sir. My name is Detective Sergeant Morris. Would you please accompany us to the station to help us with our enquiries? It's just routine at this stage, and your cooperation would be greatly appreciated.'

Fear entered each of them, as yesterday's serious transgression replayed in their minds. Each responded in quiet submission. There was absolutely no link between any of them and the unfortunate motel owner. However, they were circumspect not to say anything in the presence of a police officer and complied with the request.

They were each escorted to separate interview rooms, accompanied by a uniformed officer. The rooms were identical—four brick walls painted light green. A single light globe with no shade was hanging from the centre of the room. There were no windows, just a single door. The furniture was basic—a small square table with a chair each side. A uniformed policeman stood by the door.

Tension increased as Sergeant Morris entered the room. 'Thank you for coming in, Reverend. As you've been told, this is a routine enquiry at this stage, and we need to eliminate certain people from our enquiries before proceeding further.'

It was the first time any of them had been invited by the police for interview. Alex was more nervous because Brian wasn't with him. What was he to say?

'I'm going to ask you a few questions, and I'll write down your answers. Then I'll get your statement typed up for you to sign. It shouldn't take long, and I thank you again for coming in. Can you give me your whereabouts yesterday afternoon between three and five o'clock?' the detective asked.

Brian's throat constricted and an involuntary cough embarrassed him.

'Yes, of course,' he said as he recovered his composure. 'I was at the dean's residence, planning a Bible study group for my local parish. I arrived shortly after lunch and met a colleague, Reverend Charles Huskins. We'd planned to help each other.'

'And what time did you leave, sir?'

'Well, I had to get back to my rectory before the kids came home from school, so it would have been about four o'clock, I think.' Brian tried to sound matter of fact rather than precisely give times within three and five o'clock.

'And can anyone vouch for your timing and attendance?'

'Yes, of course. Reverend Huskins as well as the dean's wife. She was in and out of the meeting, providing tea and cakes.'

'And was there any particular reason why you didn't have the meeting at yours or Reverend Huskins's church?'

'Well, yes. I hesitate to admit, but her coffee and home-made cakes are much better than either Charles or I could have provided.' They both laughed.

'I'll get this typed up so you can sign them for the record,' said the detective. 'Officers will, of course, then corroborate your statements.'

'Yes, of course,' said Brian. 'We've nothing to hide.' *Why did I say that? Why did I say* we? *The statement was only for me?* The fear developed. This was no coincidence.

Charles was much more clinical and didn't try to make any jokes. He answered the questions in accordance with the agreed alibi, short and to the point.

Alex was nervous and kept asking for the questions to be repeated. *I can't help thinking they know something.*

They all signed their respective statements, and the detective thanked them for coming in.

'We ask your continued patience while we check these out,' said the detective, and he left them with their thoughts.

Detective Morris visited the deanery and was invited in by the dean's wife. 'My husband is still overseas on one of his lecturing tours. Please come into the lounge.'

'I need to speak with you to corroborate statements we hold for Reverend Braithwaite and Huskins on the afternoon of yesterday. They both say they were here between the hours of three and five o'clock. Can you verify that?'

'Yes, of course,' she said. 'They were preparing for a study group of some description. They used the dean's study, and I gave them refreshments during the afternoon. I can't remember what time they left, but they sure liked my cakes. I think they got through three serves of coffee and cake. They would have been here a couple of hours at least, I think. I didn't look at the clock. It was late afternoon. I'm sorry, I don't notice these things in detail.'

Without exception, everyone at the soup kitchen confirmed with the police the Reverend Alex Bates had been there all afternoon and evening.

Detective Morris interviewed several inmates. 'Were you here yesterday afternoon between three and five o'clock?'

'Oh yes,' they each replied. 'And so was the reverend, between three and five o'clock.' The story they all gave was strong and repetitious in precise detail. The detective wasn't as naive not to recognise the peculiarity of such repetitious detail. Normally, in a group of people— in this case, at least forty—the story would have varied at least in their memories of time. But not in this case, they all distinctly remembered the time, between three and five o'clock.

A few embellished their story by telling the detective the reverend was preparing their evening meal, which was a vegetable soup and a bread roll, followed by tea or coffee and a piece of fruit. 'He was also with us all night, serving us a delicious meal.' At least that part was true.

Having collaborated the statements with the alibis, a senior detective took over the interview.

'Thank you again for your patience, gentlemen. My name is Senior Detective Jonathon Keegan of local area command. We have certain procedures to go through before we take the next step. Before reading you your rights, I need your approval to record our discussion.'

THE DEAN'S WIFE AND THREE YOUNG CURATES   ~177~

Without waiting for any response, he switched on the recorder and stated his name, date and time, and listed the clergymen present.

'Do any of you gentlemen watch DVDs?'

What a strange question, thought Brian. But again, before any of them could respond, the detective clicked the remote controller on the TV, and there they all were, stars in their own reality murder show! Even though they were back views, they recognised themselves as participants in events the previous afternoon. The camera was focused on one particular area of the bed, doubtless for Dan's personal viewing. The three moved in and out of the screen, all from behind. Even though there was no full-frontal face recognition, there was no doubt in anyone's mind who they were. There was no dialogue, just visuals.

He cautioned them, saying, 'You will now be held overnight and appear before the court tomorrow for arraignment. At that time, you can make a plea and get access to legal counsel.'

The collective response: stunned silence!

CHAPTER FIFTY-FOUR

FOLLOWING ARREST, BOOKING, and the initial bail phases, the criminal process took over. Arraignment was the first stage of court procedure, during which the three charged stood in the dock, still together.

The judge read out the murder charge, asking the defendants if they had a lawyer, following which they should make a plea. 'Guilty, not guilty, or no contest?'

Silence! They were still numbed by a completely new direction their lives were heading.

'If you're not making a plea, I suggest you take legal advice. If you do not have your own council, the court will appoint one for you. Bail denied. I'll set this case aside for a preliminary hearing in fourteen days, during which I suggest you get legal advice, gentlemen. Next!' The judge moved on to the next case.

The legal counsel provided pro bono service and was usually a newly qualified and totally inexperienced lawyer. Tony Zappia, the first generation of new immigrants, was a young man just twenty-five years old, except he looked like a teenager. Consequently, apart from lacking experience, he had the distinct disadvantage of looking too young to even be in court, let alone represent three senior ministers of the church in a murder trial.

The first interview was one of introductions. Clearly, Tony was out of his depth. 'I need to know how you plan to plead.' 'How about guilty?'

Silence.

'How about not guilty?'

Silence.

'Look, I can't help you unless you talk to me. I'm sorry if I'm a bit green, but I'm all you've got. So please help me to help you.'

Silence.

Tony decided to approach a Queen's counsellor in the legal practice in which he'd become an employee. He knocked on the door while looking at the name etched on the glass door, wondering if it was mandatory to have a double-barrelled name—'Horatio Worthington-Smyth QC Barrister at Law'. As he waited, he remembered a QC was appointed by letters patent as one of the Queen's counsel, learned in law. Tony wondered if he'd ever aspire to such a high status and enter the Bar. He was wondering why becoming a QC was referred to as 'taking silk' when a voice bellowed. 'Enter.'

Having explained the extent of his knowledge of the case, Tony asked for guidance.

The QC appeared totally disinterested in the question. 'What evidence have prosecution and police presented?'

Tony offered the DVD, while giving his unlearned opinion. 'They're each as guilty as anyone could imagine.'

Worthington-Smyth viewed the DVD, steepled his fingers pointed heavenwards as if in prayer, eyes closed. 'Your job is to defend these gentlemen, not to judge them based on prosecution evidence. Have you ever conducted an identification parade where they pick a number of people off the street and put him in a line asking for a witness to recognise the guilty party?'

'No, sir, but I've seen it on TV. Seems quite straightforward.'

'Have you ever seen one where they all stood with their back to the witness?' Worthington-Smyth sounded exasperated.

Tony had to admit it did seem a bit unlikely, except this was clearly the end of the interview, as the DVD was handed back.

They didn't have to respond to Tony's questions but didn't yet understand he was their only hope of presenting any mitigating circumstances. The preliminary hearing came and went, the only evidence presented to the court at this stage was a broad outline of the case and prosecution expressing confidence claiming a guilty verdict.

They knew they were as guilty as hell but were ignorant of the process in which they'd become inextricably involved.

CHAPTER FIFTY-FIVE

EVEN THOUGH THEY'D taken the laptop and all the backup hard discs, the footage of their collective misdemeanour hadn't been downloaded from the camera's memory on to the laptop. They weren't aware a camera had captured their collective transgression as they dealt with Dan. The crime scene appeared to be beyond any reasonable doubt so far as they were concerned.

The dean's wife hadn't shared the true details of her blackmailer's demand with Brian who, as usual, had influenced Charles and Alex to join forces to deal with the problem.

The scuffle, the overpowering of Dan, and the strangulation were captured in video only because Dan had no need for audio. The camera was fixed and focused on the bed. It wasn't until Dan was put on the bed after they thought he was dead that Dan came into view. There was no way it could be suggested he was dead. The resurrection proved that, but the repeat strangulation was recorded, except it was a jumble of bodies and again without facial display.

Due to the absence of audio, there had been no reference to the dean's wife. Neither was there any record of her visits to the motel, and of course, there wasn't any hard-copy photos the dean's wife had suggested formed material for blackmail.

But to some extent, it had been Brian who'd introduced the need to do something and his motivation was self-preservation. He'd led his two friends into an inescapable situation in the same way he'd led them into ministry.

Contrary to legal advice, they decided to plead guilty and throw themselves on the mercy of the court. The reality of the world in which they lived had become the reality by which they would now be judged.

When police had checked their alibis, the dean's wife was cautioned, as she confirmed she had supported clergy in ignorance of what they might have been doing. 'I couldn't believe a clergyman would do anything illegal. You're telling me this has to do with a murder, except I knew nothing of that until you've just told me. I'm very sorry. Will I be charged?'

Sergeant Morris decided. 'I don't believe it would make any difference to the case, so I won't pursue the matter further. However, it's a very serious matter corroborating a signed statement without knowing the details of what really happened.'

It was true she didn't know there'd been a murder, and this made her feel righteous in her false confirmation that Brian and Charles were at the deanery that fateful afternoon.

The police didn't bother to revisit Alex's street people and their corroboration. It was clear they'd all lied to support the comfort and free meals they enjoyed. He couldn't blame them.

The church would have nothing to do with any defence of their ministers and took the path of least resistance, accepting guilt before trial.

The judge set aside three weeks for the trial. However, at the first court hearing, the bombshell was dropped as all three pleaded guilty. The judge called both parties' lawyers into chambers. 'What's going on here? I have set down a three-week trial, and the jury have been notified. Have your clients been advised their rights and are they simply throwing themselves on the mercy of the court? I'll have to dismiss the jury!'

The prosecution barrister interrupted. 'Your Honour, the case is indefensible. If they are going to plead guilty and my learned friend has no defence to offer to the contrary, I rest my case.'

This got up the judge's nose. 'If you don't mind, I shall decide whether the case is cut short. This is not the place to make judgement, and we need to follow due process of the law in court.'

'Certainly, and thank you, Your Honour.'

Tony thought he had to say something. 'My clients are three Anglican ministers who are suffering the shock of being charged with murder. I have made several attempts to discuss their defence, but they remain silent. Evidence in the form of camera footage appears to place them at the scene of the crime. I can only presume, in the absence of any meaningful discussion, they have decided to be seen as truthful before God.'

'Very well, Mr Zappia, I will reconvene the court and conduct the shortest murder trial in my learned experience.' His Honour was not pleased.

Back in court, the judge spoke. 'Gentlemen, you have pleaded guilty to this crime, which I have to say is the most unusual case I have ever sat in judgement. There is no known motive, you don't appear to have had any relationship with the victim, and defence is unable to offer any mitigating circumstances. At least, we have a body! Apart from your plea of guilty, do you have anything to say before I pass judgement?'

They had become adept at keeping silent. They could have said they were sorry to have brought the church into disrepute, but it never crossed their minds. Perhaps more to the point was they were sorry they'd been caught.

In the minds of the three defendants, the complexity of the case was such that to try and explain to the court would have served no useful purpose. It would also have implicated the dean's wife.

The judge dismissed the jury with apologies for bringing them into court to no avail. He then directed his attention to both legal counsellors. 'A most unusual case and definitely the shortest. I shall consider the guilty pleas in good measure of the three defendants. I will announce judgement in three weeks. Case closed.'

Dan's prediction the police might one day call upon his indiscreet footage as evidence of a crime became a truth beyond his intended purpose.

Whereas the dean's wife had encouraged the dirty deed, she'd neither instructed nor suggested they should murder Dan.

The clergymen had destroyed all the archives of incriminating footage as soon as they'd left the motel, so the police were not aware of any evidence that might have justified premeditated intent. There was no known motive, but there was a body and the irrefutable evidence recorded on the motel room camera. To all intents and purposes, any court evidence of blackmail had been destroyed and was never mentioned in court. It was simply an open-and-shut case: three clergymen had committed the crime by their own admission.

The judge passed judgement—fifteen years!

CHAPTER FIFTY-SIX

S ALLY WASN'T TOLD she'd have to leave the rectory. It was a forgone conclusion she'd worked out herself rather than have it made for her by the church in a much more prolonged, painful, and public way.

The case was not one of suspicion of having committed murder; it was a lay-down misère so far as the media were concerned. If it'd just been suspicion, it could have taken years for the church to remove her and her family from the rectory, during which time the clergymen would have been stood aside while the law took its course. However, they were legally trumped with the first hand through their own plea.

Sally had gone to live with her parents, and the church had washed their hands of her. Charles's wife, Angela, also left her rectory and returned to her parents. The church was unable to offer any help. They didn't know what to say or what to do, so they said and did nothing.

They both heard the voice of the church. 'Your husband has been found guilty, so you and your children are guilty too!'

It wasn't long before both Sally's and Angela's parents were posing the question of what their daughters planned to do. 'You can't wait fifteen years for your defrocked husband to be discharged from prison, and then what? No job, no home, no future. You have to think of the children,' her father voiced as non-negotiable advice.

Her mother quickly added, 'You can't stay here forever. Apart from anything else, what are the neighbours going to say?'

'I hadn't expected to stay here forever,' said Sally. 'But I had thought under the circumstances over which I had no control, you would have been a bit more tolerant of your grandchildren and me.'

Both mothers had to think of the kids. So Sally and Angela filed for divorce and put themselves back on the marriage market. They hadn't visited their respective husbands in prison, and the kids were simply told Daddy had gone away. They were too young to understand; there would soon be a new daddy.

CHAPTER FIFTY-SEVEN

PRISON WAS, OF course, a new experience for all three, having not even visited a prison, either as a guest or a clergyman to exercise pastoral care. Naturally they were defrocked following their convictions, and they entered the prison system through the normal process of strip search, allocation of prison clothes, a blanket and a toilet roll.

The routine was structured—even strict—but hardly austere, and the food was passable. The most difficult part was the company, as they were incarcerated with criminals and murderers! Brian set about providing advice to other inmates whose level of intelligence were a few bars below normal, although he'd often doubted his own level of intelligence after having ended up exactly where they were, in prison.

Charles just went with the flow—what else could he do? Alex fell apart not for his own discomfort or well-being but for the street-people he'd let down. The soup kitchen had been closed, and the church had nobody else to fill Alex's role.

Charles's parish hardly missed him, and he was easily replaced. Brian's parish reflected with great hindsight that they'd always thought there was something wrong with him. He was just too good to be true.

The dean returned home from overseas to be told by his wife that a terrible thing had happened in the diocese and the three young ministers had apparently murdered a motel owner.

'Why in heaven's name would they do such a thing?' asked the dean.

'I have no idea,' she replied. 'The police didn't seem to know either, but there was a camera running in the motel room where it all happened, which clearly showed the three of them caught in the act.' It was almost sufficient truth to acquiesce the dean.

'But surely the police questioned them about motive?' the dean felt need of further comment.

'No, they refused to answer any questions, and their defence counsel was unable to even present a case. Apparently they remained silent throughout the trial other than pleading guilty and threw themselves on the mercy of the Court.'

As the years slowly passed in prison, the three often reflected on how easily they'd been led astray. It wasn't simply because they were friends; they also shared issues far from any clerical training and more close to their world reality. It was the same reality with which they now viewed the outside world. Ministry appeared to offer what they thought would be an easy life, except somehow they thought they'd be insulated from worldly judgement as clergymen—not from murder, of course, but from their other collective transgressions.

The dean never visited them in prison. He'd lost his successor, so what was the point? The dean's wife made an effort to visit a couple of times to thank them discreetly for holding their counsel. She knew they could've implicated her, but she also knew she would've been on very thin ice if she'd explained the real reason behind Dan's blackmail.

CHAPTER FIFTY-EIGHT

THEIR LIVES QUICKLY settled into the expected prison drudgery, except Brian was always able to see something positive. The three ex-clergymen protected each other; Alex attended the well-equipped gymnasium every day and had developed a good relationship with other inmates, due in no small measure to his muscular physique. His physical attributes also served to protect his two associates, enabling Brian to provide advice for any situation and Charles to be a sort of go-between or secretary. Other prison inmates seemed to respect the three unusual characters, if for no other reason than they had been convicted of murder, a more serious crime than most others incarcerated with them had committed.

Many inmates were in need of counselling, with family problems going on outside prison. Brian established a counselling system. It was not possible to just turn up and consult; an appointment had to be made. Charles was part of the team by establishing a triage to gain access to Brian. It became busy, and Charles acted also as letter-writer because most of the inmates were illiterate. Letters were mostly to wives, but of course, feedback could be less than informative.

The three inmates settled into a lifestyle of compliance—once again together, though in the same prison instead of the same diocese, and still interdependent and sharing a life within their new reality.

Suddenly the dean died. A heart attack was the cause. One day he was there, and the next he was gone—quite a shock for the dean's wife. Naturally, she went through the outward grieving process. She had a sweet little black cocktail dress for the occasion. However, she soon realised (as had Sally and Angela) that she'd have to vacate her home owned by the church, as it would soon be offered to a new dean. She soon remarried to support the lifestyle to which she had become accustomed.

CHAPTER FIFTY-NINE

THE THREE EX-CLERGYMEN had been in prison for five years. Adding to it their detention prior to trial meant they had effectively served six and a half years.

They'd settled down to the routine of prison life in the realisation that it was easier to comply than to fight the system. There was no thought of escape back to the reality of their earlier world. Escape to what? This was their new reality which they'd created, so they lived in resigned acceptance. They'd each deserved the sentence, and there was no point in a legal appeal. Appeal for what? The sentence had been lenient because they pleaded guilty.

They'd each gone through their own emotional trauma coming to terms with prison life, but it had been easier doing it together. Gone were dreams about the outside world with its freedom of choice. Whereas they were not free in body, they were now free in mind. But they were not yet free in spirit.

The prison warden was a Christian, confused with the story about his three special inmates but unable to find any records to enlighten him. He didn't judge them, but he wondered how they'd come to fall from grace so dramatically. He was aware of the biblical truth of God's forgiveness available to anyone who, with contrite heart, truly sought forgiveness for his or her sins. They were model prisoners in terms of manners and compliance with regulations. They didn't fit into the normal system of prison life by virtue of their previous positions in society, but they were no trouble. Quite the contrary, they provided an internal service to fellow inmates.

Because of their personas, the warden had isolated them from the other inmates. In Christian faith, he'd wanted to reach out to them. It was beyond his comprehension they were anything but men of God. The court had exercised penal judgement, but he couldn't help having compassion for them. They seemed such nice guys. He'd formed the opinion that there must have been some hidden agenda behind their murderous action which never came out in court. He was able to justify his actions in providing them special attention and privileges as a consequence.

In prison Alex had expressed the view with his two friends that perhaps there was more to life than the world had to offer. There'd been plenty of time to share their thoughts, which at an earlier time they wouldn't have bothered. Time was now a commodity they had in abundance. These discussions took place when they'd returned to the privacy of their cells for the night. During the day, they met at meal times, but there were always plenty of inmates in earshot to discourage confidential discussion. So in the quietness of their cells, they would talk. These discussions usually took place after lights out, and they felt secure in their own little world for the night. It was an escape they almost looked forward to at the end of each day.

The three cells they'd been allocated were more comfortable than others, except they also had a special feature unknown to the occupants. These cells were used to try and get information from occupants and were wired for sound. Recordings could be taken and used as evidence, although this was not the intent of the warden with the current occupants.

He was concerned perhaps they were protecting someone who might otherwise have been implicated in the murder. The warden had nothing else to do, so he regularly listened into their evening chatter. *If only I could find the secret of what might've been withheld from the court, I might be able to make a case to the early release tribunal.*

They were model inmates. As he listened, he was alarmed to hear all three had lost their faith. Their discussions were searching for answers to the meaning of life, devoid of any spiritual understanding. Of course, what he didn't know was they'd not lost their faith; they'd never had any! As a Christian, he wondered how he could help them in their collective dilemma.

CHAPTER SIXTY

O UT OF THE blue, they had a visitor, who was, in fact, their only visitor. He'd left a card so the warden made contact and asked him to come in for a chat. He looked at the card and invited him to come and help.

'Hello, this is Fr Carlos Resendez. Can I help you?'

'Thank you,' said the warden, introducing himself. 'We have some common acquaintances—Brian, Charles, and Alex.'

'Yes,' said Carlos. 'They're actually old schoolmates, and I haven't seen them for years. I'd wondered what happened to them except my recent visit didn't throw any light on the reason.'

The warden immediately opened up a Christian dialogue. There was no need for small talk. 'I'm very concerned about their spiritual welfare and wonder if you'd come in for a chat to see if you can help.'

'Yes, of course. I've had similar concerns but have been unsuccessful in getting them to talk about it.'

When Carlos arrived, the warden shared the discreet sound link. They sat in the warden's office listening to Brian, Charles, and Alex, who were in their night cells. Both the warden and Carlos agreed they were lost souls in need of redemption.

'I've been unable to work out where these guys stand in Christ,' said the warden. 'Everything they say is so secular and devoid of anything spiritual. I realise one of them may have lost his faith after being incarcerated, but all three just doesn't make sense.'

'How about we start by just listening to what they say for a while,' said Carlos. 'You've listened to them before, so let me try and get a handle on things from a new perspective.' Carlos was rather more experienced than the warden.

After a while, Carlos came to the point. 'So what are we actually trying to achieve?'

The warden shared his opinion of trying to find out some

background that may assist his presentation to the early release tribunal. But he also wanted to release them from their unforgiveness. 'This is spiritual warfare,' said the warden.

Carlos continued, 'The problem is, people make decisions about Christianity from misinformation or even worse, no information. To a great extent, it's due to teaching colleges that, one way or another, are different. The worst thing that happened in Christendom was the Reformation, because it divided the church, Catholic and Anglican, in the sixteenth century. It has been dividing ever since. It all adds to the confusion of misinformation, and yet we all use the same Bible. We all have the same God!'

It was difficult for either of them to draw any conclusions on how these three clergymen had come to a position of such abject unbelief. However, both the warden and Carlos started from the assumption that the change was as a consequence of the murder. It was inconceivable they were like it at ordination.

The discussion they overheard was simply domestic chatter. 'There is, of course, a difference in their language compared with other prisoners. No vulgarities or swear words. They never criticise the food, the work, or the discipline,' said the warden.

Then, all of a sudden, there was a change of subject as Alex raised his hobby-horse question. 'How are we supposed to get in touch with the Holy Spirit?'

'Oh, not that again,' said Charles. 'Why do you keep harping on about the Holy Spirit. You know there isn't any such thing. We went all through all that in the seminary.'

'Yes, give it a rest,' said Brian. 'Nobody really believes in that rubbish.'

'So why did we used to say, in the name of the Father and of the Son and of the Holy Spirit?' said Alex for the umpteenth time.

The warden belonged to a charismatic church, and Carlos was liberal. Both were deeply hurt at this blasphemy, not only because they were blaspheming against the Holy Spirit, which the Bible says is an unforgivable sin, but also because they were previously ordained ministers.

'Mind you,' said Carlos, 'there would probably be other ordained ministers who would similarly deny the ministry of the Holy Spirit, except they wouldn't be as honest in declaring their disbelief.'

It was clear the three inmates were ill equipped to help each other. Consequently, their discussions went nowhere. They'd previously rejected offers to meet the prison chaplain. There wasn't a connection with him considered worthy of pursuing.

Alex had always thought there was more to the Holy Spirit issue and had visited the prison library to check out the Acts of the Apostles in the New International Version (NIV) of the Bible. Whereas his previous readings considered the matter fictional, suddenly he believed them to be true. This was a bit of a worry because he knew his cellmates would not consider any Bible text to be any different from their previous understanding.

Carlos suggested inviting Alex in for a chat to have some discussion about the Holy Spirit. There was no point including the other two at this stage because their minds were closed to anything spiritual.

CHAPTER SIXTY

ALEX WAS NOT in the least concerned about the invitation and even welcomed the opportunity to talk privately. He was however surprised to see Carlos in attendance. The warden opened the discussion without mentioning they'd listened in on the threesome's negative reference to the Holy Spirit.

The warden came straight to the point. 'We'd like to talk to you about the Holy Spirit.'

'Sure,' said Alex. 'I've wanted to talk about him ever since ordination.'

'Well, we're willing to talk about him,' said Carlos. 'But before we do, let's ask if you believe in God.'

'Yes,' replied Alex without hesitation. 'I also believe in the Holy Spirit, except nobody would ever tell me how I could get to know him. I would also like to receive a gift of the Spirit, but whenever I've spoken to anyone, they've always said the gifts were no longer available and were for apostolic times. Apparently, God withdrew them because they were no longer needed.'

A great sadness came over Carlos and the warden. They were both aware this issue was swept aside in several mainstream churches.

'We have a really good starting point,' said Carlos. 'If you'd denied either or both, we'd have to stop right there. However, since you have faith, we can continue.'

'How do you know I have faith?' asked Alex. 'I don't even know what faith is.'

'Let me put it this way,' said Carlos. 'If you believed there was no God, that would be your faith. If you believe there is a God, then that is your faith.'

'Is that all there is to faith?' asked Alex.

'No, there's a lot more to it than that, but no amount of explanation about faith will have any meaning unless you believe in God. So we have made a good start,' Carlos was able to encourage him.

'I asked my bishop about the Holy Spirit and the gifts of the Spirit, and he quoted me 1 Corinthians, Chapter 12. I've read it many times, but it never meant a thing. I always came to the conclusion it was just a biblical story and was no longer relevant.'

'I'm presuming you've had the first blessing of the Holy Spirit?' Carlos wanted to know.

Alex was confused. 'What do you mean the first blessing?'

'When you were baptised,' said Carlos.

'Yes, of course,' replied Alex. 'At least I think I was, or maybe I was just christened and given a name. If I hadn't, then my name wouldn't be Alex, would it?'

Both Carlos and the warden were bemused by the response, except their reaction was to comfort Alex.

'If there's any doubt, we will baptise you now,' said Carlos. 'Get some water please, Warden, and a Book of Common Prayer.'

'You guys don't mess around, do you?' said Alex. 'Does it matter whether I've been baptised or not?'

'Most definitely,' said Carlos. 'Even if you have been baptised, there's no harm in doing it again. And if you haven't then, you're now able to receive the Holy Spirit as your first blessing. Most people are baptised as children, and even if they're confirmed, it was such a long time ago they usually can't remember.'

They went through the rite of baptism, and Alex received the first blessing of the Holy Spirit willingly and fully.

Then Carlos explained the biblical narratives of the second blessing of the Holy Spirit, which was just as available today as it ever had been. 'The Bible is the written word of God, in which it doesn't say anywhere that the Holy Spirit has been or ever will be withdrawn. Let's move on. The Holy Spirit is the third person of the Holy Trinity. God is three persons in one—God the Father, God the Son, and God the Holy Spirit.'

'Wow!' said Alex. 'Fantastic. Why couldn't somebody have told me that before? Where is he now?'

'Good question,' replied Carlos. 'The first person of the Holy Trinity, God the Father has always been in existence. Before time, even before creation, because God created everything seen and unseen. God the Father exists outside time and space, was and is still and forever will be. Both Jesus and the Holy Spirit were there with the Father before creation.'

'How do you know all this stuff?' asked Alex.

Carlos thought but couldn't say, *How is it you don't you know all this stuff? Have you never read John's Gospel?*

Carlos continued, 'God the Son, Jesus, came to earth about two thousand years ago to live and experience our human life. As you know, he died and rose again, returning to the heavenly places, where he now sits at the right hand of the Father. Jesus is our advocate who ever intercedes for us, which is why we always say in prayer 'through Jesus Christ, our Lord'. After Jesus was crucified, died, and rose again, he appeared to his disciples, but before he returned to the heavenly places, he said he would send us a comforter, a counsellor, and he is the third person of the Holy Trinity—the Holy Spirit. The Holy Spirit first came on the Day of Pentecost, and he's still here.'

Alex was close to tears, thinking, *Why on earth didn't they teach us this at the seminary?* 'So how do I get to meet him?' Alex asked through his tears.

'Simple,' said Carlos. 'We just have to invite him into our lives, into our bodies, and we do it in prayer. The Bible says our body is the temple of the Holy Spirit.'

'But I've done a terrible thing,' said Alex. 'And I can't tell you anything about it.'

'You don't have to,' said Carlos. 'It's between you and God. It's not our role to judge you, but we can act in accordance with God's word in the Bible and ask God's forgiveness. If you approach God in prayer with a contrite heart and ask his forgiveness, I have the authority to absolve you from your sin. The Bible says if you do this, God will see your sin no more. The Bible also says instead of your sins being as scarlet, they will be as white as snow.'

'How long will all this take?' asked Alex, thinking it might take years.

'Only a few moments, and we can do it now, before you go back to your cell.'

Alex thought for a while of Brian and Charles. 'What about my two friends? Will the Holy Spirit be available to them as well? Can we pray for them to be absolved or whatever you called it?'

'Unfortunately, no,' said Carlos. 'Your friends have to have faith. They have to believe in God. Otherwise, prayer will just be empty words.'

Alex knew this was a problem with them and felt guilty being offered absolution without his two friends. 'OK,' said Alex, 'let's pray. Please also pray I'll receive a gift of the Spirit.'

Carlos and the warden laid hands on Alex, joining in faith together. They prayed. 'Loving and heavenly Father, we stand together in faith and believe for our brother in Christ, Alex.' They shared the words from St John's Gospel. '"If anyone sins, we have an advocate with the Father, Jesus Christ the righteous, and he is the perfect offering for our sins . . ."'

'Alex seeks forgiveness for acts committed in his past life, about which only you and he knows.'

Carlos then asked Alex to repeat some words, of which he was very familiar, except he was now to say them in the first person.

'Merciful God, my Maker and my Judge, I have sinned against you in thought, word, and deed. I have not loved you with my whole heart. I have not loved my neighbour as myself. I repent and am sorry for all my sins. Father, forgive me. Strengthen me to love and obey you in newness of life, through Jesus Christ, my Lord. Amen,'

Carlos then pronounced absolution.

'Almighty God, who has promised forgiveness to all who turn to him in faith, pardon you and set you free from all your sins, strengthen you to do his will, and keep you in eternal life, through Jesus Christ, our Lord, Amen.'

'I feel as if a great burden has been lifted off me,' said Alex. 'But what was all that about newness of life?'

'We shall now pray for you to receive the second blessing of the Holy Spirit', said Carlos, 'because through his ministry you will be a new creation in Christ.'

They laid hands on Alex again.

'Come, Holy Spirit,' said Carlos, and Alex collapsed on the floor like a sack of coal. Both the warden and Carlos were familiar with people being slain in the Spirit, so they weren't concerned and left him lying on the floor. They knew he could be down for quite a while, so they offered a prayer of thanksgiving and relaxed with a cup of coffee.

About twenty minutes later, Alex started to get up. He had no idea where he was, but he was crying openly, without embarrassment.

'I met him,' said Alex. 'I met the Holy Spirit, and he told me how much God loves me, how much I've been forgiven, and he told me he'd been waiting for me to invite him into my life.'

The warden escorted Alex back to his cell since he'd lost all sense of direction.

'What happened to you?' asked Charles, but Alex didn't hear his friend. He just lay on his bunk and fell immediately into a sound sleep.

The next morning, Charles tried again. 'What happened to you last night?'

'Nothing,' replied Alex.

'Getting all secretive now, are we?'

'There's no point, you wouldn't believe me, so there's no point telling you,' said Alex.

Brian and Charles noticed a change in Alex which they couldn't explain. He was more assertive, more decisive, untroubled by anything. Alex always had something to worry about and share with his friends, but not today. He wanted to tell them because he knew the benefit, but it was too new an experience for him to share, let alone try and convert his friends. He asked the warden if he and Carlos would talk to Brian and Charles and see if they could lead them in the same way they'd led him.

CHAPTER SIXTY-TWO

T HE WARDEN AND Carlos decided on a different approach to Brian and Charles because they were more intellectual. Carlos started by appealing to their cerebral persona. There was little point in trying to approach their spiritual persona because neither Brian nor Charles was in the slightest bit spiritual.

As the warden had a close and friendly relationship with the clergymen, the suggestion of a friendly chat was welcomed. What else was there to do?

Carlos had dealt with this type of issue many times in his own church. The warden much less so, but he was willing to learn.

He started by asking Brian, 'Do you believe Julius Caesar lived at a time in history on or about two thousand years ago?'

'Of course,' replied Brian, and Charles agreed.

'What is the basis of your belief?'

'History has been written and records many stories of his leadership,' said Brian. 'I have no reason to doubt the record to be less than accurate.'

'Do you believe a man called Jesus lived at the same time?' enquired Carlos.

'No, I don't,' said Brian. Charles remained silent.

'I'm challenging the reason why you believe Caesar lived based on historical records, his life and battles, but you don't believe a man called Jesus lived, even though his life and battles were also recorded in history.'

'OK,' said Brian. 'I see what you're going with this. It's not that I don't believe the recorded history of both men who lived at the same time. What I don't believe are the things Jesus was supposed to have done.'

'Well, that's a very different position to take,' said Carlos, letting him dwell upon his thoughts a few moments.

'On the basis you now believe Jesus lived, do you believe he went into the synagogue and knocked all the tables over because people were selling things inside the synagogue?'

Brian wasn't slow on picking up the direction this was leading and said, 'I know there are many things he did and said which are probably true. So I'm prepared to agree he lived and did and said many things, some of which might be true.'

'On what basis do you accept things Caesar said and did, but not Jesus?' asked Carlos. 'History is history. You have to have a reason why you would accept one and not the other. They were both just human beings, weren't they?'

Brian was being drawn in. 'History also suggests Jesus performed a number of so-called miracles, which defy logic.'

'Well, we're all agreed then,' said Carlos. 'Jesus lived, said, and did a lot of things and performed miracles which defied logic, all recorded in history.'

'What—you agree the miracles defied logic?' said Brian.

'Of course they defied logic, otherwise they wouldn't have been miracles,' replied Carlos. He decided to take a different direction for a while. 'If you knew anything about physics and the relative position of the planets in the universe, you'd know earth is positioned in a unique way in relation to all the other planets. It's beyond logic how they all exist, and yet only earth has the ability to support life as we know it. Let me approach this from a different perspective. If I were a botanist, I could give you a similar presentation about millions of flora and fauna that exist on this planet. Similarly, in the oceans and in the air we breathe, there are microorganisms of living species all surviving in harmony that we can't see, and yet many defy logic. What I'm saying, Brian and Charles, is that just because we don't understand something— just because we don't see something or believe its illogical—does not mean it doesn't exist.'

'OK,' said Charles, 'you're appealing to our sense of logic. All those issues are acceptable, but what do they have to do with God?'

'They have everything to do with God,' said Carlos. 'Can you explain any of them from your logic?'

'Of course not, but we still don't understand how you can have a relationship with someone you can't see. It's illogical.'

'Well, you can't have it both ways,' said Carlos. 'You either accept there are things in this world you don't understand because they are illogical and you can't see them, or you're prepared to accept there might be some things you don't understand or see but they still exist.'

Brian and Charles felt they were up against a worthy challenger in their friend who suddenly took yet another approach.

'Have you ever wondered why we're here, or considered the part of you that seeks foundational thoughts? The whole of the human race has had such thoughts and sought enlightenment since creation. This part of our humanity is our spiritual persona.'

'Yes, of course,' said Brian. 'It doesn't make us Christian though.'

'True,' said Carlos. 'But if you accept the concept, then humankind is a combination of a body, mind, and spirit. You might think of spirit as being your soul. No other creature on earth has the ability to reason. We can consider our thoughts, our actions, and reason the consequences. If we proceed with those thoughts or actions, we accept the consequences and can choose to be accountable.'

The warden sent them back to their cells to dwell on the discussion they'd had with Carlos. They planned to take it further with Brian and Charles when they'd had some time to think.

CHAPTER SIXTY-THREE

CARLOS REFLECTED ON their progress. 'These two young men have been through the system of teaching religion in a totally cerebral way. We have to spend some time nurturing them towards accepting there's a spiritual side to their existence. Alex already knew he had a spiritual side and had been craving to gain access to it for many years. His willingness was overwhelmingly powerful in his conversion. We didn't have to do anything other than pray him into the kingdom, and the Holy Spirit took over. Brian and Charles are a different kettle of fish. Any effort to try and convert them will be of no consequence if they don't believe in God, because without belief, they will depend entirely on their brain for information. They've been programmed by an intellectual church. That's what I mean by cerebral knowledge,' explained Carlos.

As they thought about what Carlos had told them, Brian and Charles changed from being atheists to sceptics, except they'd absolutely no credible argument to offer themselves for their scepticism.

Alex was delighted because he now understood what the gifts of the Spirit were all about and anyone, even he, could ask God for one of the gifts. While his two friends were out of their cells visiting the warden and Carlos, Alex got down on his knees to pray. He thought this was how it was done. He silently asked God for a gift of the Spirit, believing it in his heart, and ended with *amen*.

He was unable to remember the next morning whether he dreamed about God's response or if it actually happened. It didn't matter because God's response was now indelibly imprinted in his spirit.

'My dear son, I blessed you with a gift of the Spirit many years ago. It was the gift of compassion for the unlovely in the world. You fed them, you clothed them, you provided them with shelter on those cold winter nights. You stood up for them when nobody else would, not even my church.'

He didn't share his experience with his two friends, but he did tell them he believed God had much more to show them if they were willing.

'Willing to what?' they asked.

'Willing to change, I guess, from the way you've denied God for your own personal gratification or pride,' said Alex from his new creation.

Carlos spent more time speaking to Brian and Charles over the following weeks and guided them in the ways of righteousness. Charles wanted to know what it meant to be righteous. Carlos explained how anyone could come into a right relationship with God, but it was impossible through human effort.

'We can only become righteous through Jesus because of what he's done,' said Carlos. 'And that's why Jesus came.'

'What do you mean, 'what he's done'?' said Charles.

Carlos had been waiting a long time to share the Good News with his prospective convertees. 'Jesus's life and ministry was all about showing mankind how to live in God's created world. There are many Christians who think Jesus performed miracles, healed people, and did other miracles for his sake, but in fact he did these things to show everyone the power of God. Jesus was man, and as man, he had absolute belief in the power of God. So Jesus called upon the power of God to perform all those miracles. There's a very significant quote from the Bible, John 14:12–14, in which Jesus is teaching his disciples. He refers to having faith.

'"I tell you the truth, anyone who has faith in me will do what I've been doing. He will do even greater things than these, because I am going to the Father. And I will do whatever you ask in my name, so that the Son may bring glory to the Father. You may ask for anything in my name, and I will do it," Jesus said.'

Both the warden and Carlos eventually learnt all three had come through the institution of church training for their own personal reasons and not as would have been expected—to serve God. This had been a tremendous break in confidence, but they'd agreed to take this step because at last they'd understood the error of their secular ways in their old world.

The final step before Brian and Charles's conversion was to accept God and accept Jesus the Son of God. The most difficult thing for them to accept was the person of the Holy Spirit. Alex helped by sharing his experience not only in receiving the Holy Spirit but also having received a gift of the Spirit.

At long last, Brian and Charles were willing to lay down their old personas and succumb to the will of God. Carlos and the warden prayed them into the kingdom and also invited the Holy Spirit into their lives. It was an emotional experience as they both sought God's forgiveness for their sins.

The warden and Carlos had passed wondering about the reason behind the murder of Dan, the motel owner. It was much more important that they led these three lost souls through forgiveness because, ultimately, their salvation depended on it.

Eventually Brian and Charles agreed they were willing and wanted to do it.

'Do you remember the very first question you asked me, Brian, about faith, and I said it all hangs on God?'

'Yes, I most certainly do,' said Brian.

'Well, this is going to be the same. As we go through this process of asking God's forgiveness, it will have no effect unless you believe in God. Words will be meaningless unless you believe. Then there is no limit to how God will bless you. He will forgive you and fulfil his biblical promise of salvation.'

'What does that mean?' asked Charles.

'Salvation means we are saved from many other things which the Bible refers to as being destructive in our earthly lives.'

'Sounds good!' said Charles.

'It is good,' said Carlos. 'It's the Good News of the Bible. The Christian is saved from being separated from God, our fallen human nature, and sickness and infirmity. We can be saved from many things in our human lives because God's kingdom isn't only in heaven but also on earth. It is also within you, the Bible says.'

Brian and Charles went through the process, repeating the words

Carlos led them to speak, and when they'd finished, they exercised the holy rite of absolution.

'You are now set free from sin and can move forward in your relationship with God. There is now nothing to stop you from becoming righteous,' declared Carlos.

He also explained. 'As Christians, we're all in need of regular forgiveness as we live in the real world in which there are many transgressions to lead us astray.'

Carlos reinforced the importance of celebrating Holy Communion because there were at least two sins every Christian committed regularly. 'We haven't loved our heavenly Father with all our heart and all our soul or spirit, and we haven't loved our neighbour as ourselves.'

But this was for the future. A major bridge had been crossed, and the warden greatly appreciated Carlos's ministry in bringing his three special inmates into the kingdom of God.

CHAPTER SIXTY-FOUR

THEIR EVENINGS TOGETHER after lights out now became a time of prayer, mainly in praise and thanksgiving for having been set free from sin, which had imprisoned them spiritually.

As their prayers developed, they believed nothing was impossible for God, and their prayers included being set free from physical incarceration. The life sentence meted out was fifteen years, with parole set at twelve years. They had been in for nearly seven, or about halfway. They asked God if there was anything he could do through Jesus Christ, their Lord.

Unbeknown to them, the warden had researched the prospect of applying for early release. He shared this with Carlos. 'I don't want to raise their hopes before having some response from the tribunal. The law can give permission for early release on licence and take into consideration offender's exceptional circumstances, which might justify consideration. The arbiter is the attorney general, and I've submitted claims on their behalf. I can, of course, vouch for their exceptional circumstances.'

The warden went on to explain to Carlos. 'In the Act, exceptional circumstances are generally intended to cover matters that occur after a prisoner has been sentenced. They may include extensive cooperation with enforcement officers, excellent conduct, remorse, or contrition— even acknowledgement of guilt, except they had all pleaded guilty at trial.' The warden was passionate about getting his star inmates released because he couldn't justify their incarceration any longer. 'Under subsection 19AP(5), I've discovered, the attorney general could take into account significant changes in compliant behaviour. These gentlemen have been perfect prisoners from the start, showed remorse as well as contrition, and are most unlikely to reoffend.'

Carlos could only agree.

Behaviour and conduct were all credited off the parole period, and the result was they could be released almost immediately. They were invited to the warden's meeting room where they'd met Carlos. The greeting was smiles and hugs as they were offered coffee.

The warden couldn't contain himself any longer. 'I've been working on your early release applications and am delighted to inform you that you are to be released from prison almost immediately.'

Alex looked upwards, eyes closed. 'Thank you, Father. Thank you, Jesus. Thank you, Holy Spirit.'

The news quickly travelled through the prison grapevine, and there was much excitement from the inmates. During their time in prison, the three had built up an intimate relationship with every prisoner, who each had their own story of innocence or justification. These relationships were confidential between Brian, Charles, or Alex, and the warden permitted the three ex-clergymen free access around the prison to say goodbye. It was an emotional experience for everyone, not least for the guards. Never before had this happened, and the likelihood of it ever happening again was beyond anyone's expectation.

'Is this really happening?' said Charles. 'It feels like a wonderful dream. I hope I don't wake up soon.'

Finally, they said their farewells to Carlos and the warden. They left prison together, three friends so different and yet so much the alike, except now they had a spiritual thread bonding their relationship. They'd been transformed in prison, not because of anything they'd learnt at theological college. They always knew they could fool theological college—even their bishop, their archbishop, and their congregations—but now they knew they couldn't fool God!

Brian felt the need to say something to continue the threesome relationship. 'So what do three defrocked clergymen do when they come out of prison? What does one defrocked clergyman do when he comes out of prison?'

They were aware they couldn't revisit past relationships. The church wouldn't have them back, and their parents were no longer alive. Brian and Charles were unable to visit their ex-wives, who were now remarried, and Brian's children had a new father. The very thought of this dulled their spirits as Brian realised his offspring would be forever wanting to know their paternal father. In a child's mind, they would not accept the circumstances that caused the marriage breakdown, and as they grew up, they'd probably deny their father could have done anything wrong. They'd be searching for the rest of their lives with a terrible void in their heart. It grieved Brian beyond measure, and Charles and Alex felt the hurt almost as much for them.

They decided to stop off at the Pig and Whistle for old times' sake—en route to where, they didn't know. They'd truly become street people, with nowhere to live, no job, no prospects, nobody to love them, and nobody for them to love. Their families, the church, as well the wider community rejected them. Society had no place for them. The reality of their world collapsed around them as they came to accept the enormity of the consequences of their sudden release from prison.

The Pig and Whistle looked the same both inside and out, but the barman they used to know was no longer there, and a young girl serving was not interested in anything other than serving them a beer.

'Yes?' she said. No welcoming words with a smile like, 'Hello, gentlemen, what would you like to drink.' Just a surly 'Yes?' with the inference, *What do you want? You're disturbing me.*

How things had changed! But of course, they'd changed as well. They asked around the pub if anyone knew of a church providing any food or shelter, but the response was negative. Nobody wanted to know them. But now they had a resource they never had before, as they turned not to the world for comfort but to God.

As they were finishing their beer, a man in uniform approached them and offered them somewhere to sleep for the night and a meal—the Salvation Army!

EPILOGUE

A LTHOUGH FOR SOME the story had ended, for others their story had hardly begun. The effects on extended family had been horrendous—such was life.

Brian's children were now teenagers. Nicholas was nearly fifteen; Georgina, thirteen. Sally had been remarried for seven years before the inevitable divorce became absolute. The remarriage of convenience had been a big mistake.

As the children grew up, she was determined to escape the relationship as soon as possible. For him it provided a bed partner, a housekeeper, and a cook. For her, a roof over her head and her children, but with an increasingly stressful relationship triggered when everyone was together in the company of the 'provider', life was unbearable. For Georgina, it was an inescapable infringement on her privacy as she entered puberty; and for Nicholas, his stepfather was no more than a landlord.

There was continuous discontent in the family. Nicholas developed a deep hatred for his stepfather and fantasised relieving his mother from her terrible burden. He drew comfort by thinking how he could get rid of him. *Perhaps Dad had similar thoughts in his misdemeanour.*

His sister had always accepted her real father was a murderer. She would never forgive him. He was responsible for the dreadful life she and her mother endured. The final straw had been when Georgina started to develop as a young woman and her stepfather entered the bathroom as she was coming out of the shower. His justification was that it was his house and his bathroom to which he could come and go as he pleased. In this respect, he was rather like Dan, the motel owner.

Even though Nicholas and Georgina were told the same story, they'd drawn very different conclusions of reality. Nicholas often asked his mother if they could visit their father in prison, but it was always denied.

Nicholas felt so empty, so unworthy, and he missed his father desperately and decided to track him down when he'd been released from prison. Love can be a peculiar emotion, because in Nicholas it had developed out of hope and expectation rather than the reality his sister endured. Georgina's hatred developed in a negative way.

Nicholas started his search at the church, but Brian's bishop was no longer alive. He spoke to the new bishop, explaining he'd not seen his father since he was about five and had little or no recollection of him. The response was sympathetic although not very helpful.

'The record shows Revd Brian Braithwaite had been very successful at St Aiden's as well as further afield in public life. There was no suggestion of impropriety.' The bishop was as confused as Nicholas.

'Then why did he kill the motel owner?'

'I have no idea.'

Nicholas reflected on his mother's knowledge of Dan's murder. He'd always thought she was being secretive, but perhaps she knew nothing either. The next step was to visit the prison and speak with the warden.

'Your father was a model prisoner. I couldn't speak more highly of him,' the warden was happy to divulge. 'I suggest you contact the Salvation Army, which has records of ex-prisoners. It's often the first place they know where to get help.'

At the army HQ, Nicholas asked if he could see Brian Braithwaite and was surprised to be told he could see him almost immediately. Nicholas was shown into an office. The Salvation Army officer was in his uniform, and they shook hands.

'And what can I do for you, young man?' said Brian.

'Hi, Dad,' was all Nicholas could say, and the two of them went into a bear hug, both shedding tears of joy. Neither could break the moment or the embrace, and it lasted several minutes. When eventually they parted, the emotions flooded out again.

'I am so pleased to see you, so pleased. I'm unable to tell you how pleased I am. The unlikelihood of this meeting has been eating away in my heart for years,' said Brian.

Nicholas's intent was to find out what happened all those years ago, but suddenly it wasn't important any more. The tears had ceased, and they were both smiling. Brian found himself looking at himself in the mirror as a young man. Where had all those wasted years gone?

Without thinking about what he was saying, Nicholas said, 'Come home, Dad. We need you.'

'It's not possible, son. Too much hurt has been inflicted and too many lives spoiled as a consequence of my actions.'

Brian was surprised to hear his son say, 'Forgiveness heals the mind as well as the spirit and sometimes even the body.'

Brian didn't need to be told that, but his son was correct. 'Perhaps one day, your mum might find it in her heart to forgive me.'

Nicholas then asked his burning question. 'Dad, did you actually murder someone?'

Brian looked deep into his son's eyes and knew the time had come to share his burden of past guilt. Nicholas also knew whatever his father was about to tell him would be the truth.

'No, I didn't actually murder him, but I was complicit. The three of us acted in premeditated murder, for which we pleaded guilty and were sentenced.'

'But why, Dad?'

Brian explained truthfully, 'The motel keeper had been blackmailing the dean's wife in the diocese in which we were all clergymen. She didn't ask us to murder him. She asked for our help, but we were young and immature, having perhaps seen too many murder movies. Blackmailers don't give up, and we decided to deal with it in a finite way.'

'But why didn't you tell the court. They could've considered mitigating circumstances, and the motive may have been justified to some extent?'

Brian was quiet for a while and said, 'It wouldn't have made any difference. We killed the guy. We were guilty, so why involve the dean's wife? It wouldn't have influenced the court. We were protecting the dean's wife as well as our own interests, as we were just starting in our church careers. I was even being groomed to be the next dean. Thank God that never happened.'

Brian hadn't told any lies, but he'd kept secret the relationship he and his two friends had with the dean's wife. It would have served no useful purpose then—not for him, not for his son, not for his ex-wife, and certainly not for the dean's wife. That part had never changed. If there was ever to be reconciliation with his wife and daughter, the complete story would remain a secret to his grave.

'So what are you doing in uniform with the Salvation Army, Dad?' Nicholas asked with a tearless grin on his face.

'What do you think a defrocked clergyman could do after he came out of prison?' They both laughed until they cried again and embraced in another timeless bear hug.

When he left, he went to his mother's house to try and get them to forgive. He explained his meeting with his father, but it was as if they weren't listening. They wanted to hold on to their hurt—their unforgiveness. Nicholas could see it was destroying them emotionally and despaired at their unwillingness to choose a different direction in life. They were so negative about their past as well as their future, except they did have a choice. It wasn't that they chose to be unhappy; they were unable to see things in the same way as Nicholas.

Georgina wanted everything to be restored from unhappiness to happiness immediately, and because she considered this to be impossible, it was a no-brainer for her even to consider. 'It's all right for you,' she said to Nicholas. 'It hasn't affected you. Look at Mum and me. We're both nervous wrecks!'

Nicholas thought about it for a while and said, 'It's not that it hasn't affected me. I don't dwell on the negative issues all the time. My glass is always half-full, yours is always half-empty.'

Georgina's response as her tears started to flow was to seek her mother's shoulder to cry on, saying, 'It's all Dad's fault.'

Nicholas realised he was unable to encourage them to see things objectively. He also understood how easy it was to blame someone else. He knew it wasn't Georgina's fault. But she did have a choice, and she was choosing to live in the past. Both Georgina and his mother had been judgemental from the very beginning, whereas Nicholas didn't believe his father had actually murdered someone. Now he knew he'd been correct.

A day arrived in Georgina's life that she'd been dreading for as long as she could remember. Her mother died! Now she had no one's shoulder to cry on, no one with whom she could commiserate about how hard her life had been. Her life had been empty. She was scared of the opposite sex and had very few friends.

She'd always lived in the shadow of her father's misdemeanour, with unforgiveness in her heart. She'd never realised what a destructive force unforgiveness had been to influence her and her mother's entire life.

Nicholas had organised and paid for his mum's funeral. Georgina didn't even know there was a cost. She thought funerals were something the church did as a service to the community. There were few guests— the prison warden together with Carlos and, of course, Nicholas and Georgina.

Out of respect for Georgina and not to upset her, Brian hadn't attended the funeral. If he'd attended, she would have said, 'How dare you come after everything you've done to us?' Because he didn't attend, she said, 'Typical, couldn't even come and pay his respects.'

After the service, the minister chatted with Nicholas and Georgina, but not together because there seemed to be some sibling friction between them. He wondered how they could have ended up so different and yet experienced the same family environment. In a sensitive way, he broached the subject and was surprised at their response because they both said exactly the same thing: 'Well, what would you expect with a father like mine?'

THE COVER STORY

THE COVER IMAGES denote the central characters in the story. The dean's wife leads the three young curates into her life of sexual gratification. This is represented by the dog collars. The clerical 'dog collars' signify an outward sign of church ethics except these are not spiritually understood by many, least of all the fictitious characters, demonstrated by their secular lifestyle.

Events take place towards the end of the twentieth century in the diocese of a major city, which could be anywhere in the Western Christian world. It's a torrid tale of questionable ethics, seduction and sexual excess, leading to crime and finally spiritual redemption. The church embedded includes the body of the church as well as the hierarchy of the Institution.

Their lives appear acceptable in a church lacking accountability. Sin is an acceptable indiscretion, not just for themselves, but also for those with whom they associate both inside the church as well as in the wider community. The young men don't consider themselves sinless, they simply have their own understanding of a world in which anything biblically sinful does not apply today. Their understanding of Christianity overlooks the difference between judgment by man rather than judgment by God. The story shows a side of Christianity, which is more about 'churchianity' meaning those who consider themselves Christian simply because they attend church on Sunday, but live a secular lifestyle from Monday to Saturday.

As the story unfolds it becomes evident the seemingly Christian structure of society is inextricably interwoven with the secular, so much so it becomes difficult to discern one from the other. This reality is shown in the fictitious character's behavior, whose experience leads them to transgressions with serious consequences. These affect not only immediate and extended family, but also subsequent generations. As the story unfolds, church and secular transgressions show how man (and woman) can momentarily fall, followed by a lifetime of anxiety, emotional pain, and even physical illness.

www.ingramcontent.com/pod-product-compliance
Lightning Source LLC
Chambersburg PA
CBHW061617100726
47898CB00002B/705